RIDING OUT THE STORM

RIDING
OUT
THE
STORM

SIS DEANS

Henry Holt and Company
New York

Henry Holt and Company, LLC
Publishers since 1866
175 Fifth Avenue
New York, New York 10010
macteenbooks.com

Henry Holt® is a registered trademark of Henry Holt and Company, LLC.

Library of Congress Cataloging-in-Publication Data
Deans, Sis Boulos.
Riding out the storm / Sis Deans.—1st ed.
p.   cm.
Summary: While riding a bus with his grandfather from Portland, Maine, to
New Jersey to visit his older brother in a mental hospital, thirteen-year-old Zach
meets some interesting people, including one very special girl.
ISBN 978-0-8050-9355-1 (hc)
[1. Interpersonal relations—Fiction.   2. Bus travel—Fiction.   3. Brothers—
Fiction.   4. Mental illness—Fiction.   5. Grandfathers—Fiction.]   I. Title.
PZ7.D3514Rid 2012
[Fic]—dc23
2011026940

First Edition—2012 / Designed by Véronique Lefèvre Sweet
Printed in the United States of America

1 3 5 7 9 10 8 6 4 2

I dedicate this book to the late Upton Brady, who took my writing and career to new heights, and whose literary wisdom and wry sense of humor I sorely miss.

RIDING
OUT
THE
STORM

CHAPTER 1

When I grow up, I'm gonna be a millionaire. If you got money, no one gives you grief. You can buy what you want, be what you want, live how you want. You got money, you don't hafta wait in line for hours, days, and freakin' months before you can get your brother help, don't hafta live wondering if he's gonna go off on you 'cause he don't like the look on your face. Don't hafta watch him lose it in public or listen to him yell and break things all day long or be afraid 24/7 'cause yuh know he's mental enough to hurt you, or himself.

That's what I'm thinking about while me and Gramp are sitting on the Greyhound bus waiting to leave Portland. Thinking how it's all about money—havin' it, makin' it, losing it. If it weren't for *That Thievin' Insurance Company*, as Ma likes to call it, my parents wouldn't have lost our house on Douglas Street, wouldn't have gone broke paying Derek's doctor bills, wouldn't have had to make him a Ward of the State justa get him help.

Weren't for *That Thievin' Insurance Company*, who only cares about makin' money and has a lifetime price tag on mental illness so they can get rid of yuh quick as they can, Derek wouldn't be a Ward of the State, and I'd still be his brother, not a *visitor* who's gotta get *special permission* just to see him.

Weren't for *That Thievin' Insurance Company*, I wouldn't be on this stinkin' bus going to New Jersey, where Derek's new parents—the State of Maine—have shipped him off to 'cause it's cheaper, 'cause it's all about money, no matter freakin' what.

And weren't for *That Thievin' Insurance Company*, I'd be playing in the basketball tournament with my eighth-grade travel team, who ain't gonna win without me, instead of sittin' here next to Gramp, who's pointing one of his sausage fingers past my nose.

"That used to be Union Station," he tells me, like it's important.

I don't say nothing 'cause who cares? But obviously Gramp

does; he's leaning right into me now so he can see out the window and over the snowbanks.

"It looked like a castle," he says. "All stone. Had a tower with a clock big enough to see what time it was when you were up on the Western Prom."

I catch a whiff of his cigar breath and just about puke. No way I can take that smell for five hundred miles, probably suffocate before we cross the bridge to South Portland.

"Idiots tore it down back in the sixties. Now look at it— Goodwill and a Dollar Store." He shakes his hairy white head like he can't believe it, whispers, "A Burger King."

"Like to sit by the window, Gramp?"

He looks at me, and those bushy eyebrows that Derek calls *albino caterpillars* meet in the middle. "No, no, Zach. I want you to have the window so you can see." He sits back and picks up the newspaper from his lap, holds it up like the news in the *Press Herald*'s some big deal. "I have this to read."

I kinda feel sorry for him, tell him, "We can take turns."

"Sure," he answers, but I know he's just saying that. He won't switch with me. The whole time we ride the dog down to New Jersey, I'll be sitting in the good seat. Still, it don't really matter, won't be able to see much; it's already getting dark out. Just one of the reasons I hate winter in Maine: looks like

3

midnight by four in the afternoon. When I grow up, I'm gonna live someplace where it's always sunny and warm. None of this snow, sleet, freezing-cold crap for me. No more of that gray-ugly sky day after day, week after week, five months long. That's why I'm hoping it's a lot warmer in New Jersey, hoping they don't get as much snow as we do, 'cause Derek only tries suicide in the winter. It's really scary to see your brother's blood all over the bathroom, but it's even scarier thinking next time he tries to slice his wrists with an X-Acto knife, Dad won't be there to break the lock on the door or Ma to call the ambulance. Now that he's a Ward of the State, we probably won't even know about it till the next day.

"Let's get this show on the road," says Gramp.

"I know," I tell him. I'm sick of waiting, too. Ma had to drop us off a whole hour early for it's "first come, first served" when you're riding the dog. Don't matter if you bought your ticket two weeks ago; you ain't in line early, you're outta luck if there's forty-seven people ahead of you, even if they bought their tickets two minutes before you got there. What sucks is, there are still some empty seats on the bus, so me and Gramp got here early for nothing.

Know what makes it worse? Soon as we saw the bus drive up, everyone ran outside like the place was on fire—some lady luggin' a pillow, hip-checking me with her luggage just to nab her "first come, first served" spot along the yellow metal railing—so I stood outside fifteen minutes freezing my butt off and breathing cigarette smoke and bus fumes for nothing, too.

"Seat's comfortable," says Gramp.

I kneel on mine, start checking things out: big windows but no way to open them; no cup holder for my Mountain Dew; over our seats, reading lights that work and two circle things you gotta twist, one for heat, one for a fan.

"Look, Gramp. There's an escape hatch in the ceiling. 'Emergency Exit. Pull Handle Fully and Push Here.' That's cool."

"Good to know," he says. "But hope we don't have to use it."

I watch the Vietnamese guy, who had an army of relatives waiting in the station with him just to say good-bye, try to shove his suitcase in the overhead rack. "No way that's gonna happen," I tell Gramp, and I'm right. The shelf's too narrow, and those thin black ropes can't stretch far enough to hold that sucker in place. Don't understand the man's language, but got a good idea what he's saying as he drags his bag back down the aisle. It's hilarious, the little wheels on his suitcase sound just as ticked off as he is, they're justa hummin' against that gray ribbed floor.

"He should have listened to the driver," says Gramp. "He told him it wouldn't fit."

I watch the guy disappear out the door, then start reading the signs up front by the driver's seat.

Fire Extinguisher under #2 RH seat
First Aid Kit—LH Parcel Rack
Fuses—Left side of Driver

WATCH YOUR STEP / CAMINE CON CUIDADO

For Passenger Safety Federal Law Prohibits Operation of
This Bus While Anyone Is Standing Forward of the White Line.

I sit back down, wondering if the Plexiglas that separates the driver's seat from the one right behind him is bulletproof. If it isn't, why's it there? So he don't get bugs? That's why Ma made me wear a hat, said, *You never know what kind of scumbag might have sat in the seat before you.* Told me, *That's how Amy's daughter got them, riding a bus to Waterville. So you keep that hat on your head, Zach, I don't want to go through that nightmare again.*

Me neither. Thanks to Derek, I know what it feels like to get your head burned off with that shampoo. Second grade, he brought home bugs three times from Mrs. Cushman's class.

"Finally," says Gramp, and as soon as he says it, the bus

driver, who looks older than Dumbledore, gets on a mic and starts ripping off rules: No smoking or drinking alcohol. Be respectful of your fellow passengers. Silence your cell phones—stuff like that. When he says, "You've rented a seat on the bus, you haven't rented the bus, and you haven't rented me," Gramp and most of the older people laugh, but when he says, "The bathroom is at the rear of the bus," the only one laughing is me.

No one thinks that's hilarious?

Derek would; he'd get it. When he's in one of his good moods, he's wicked funny. He's great at imitating people and can do any accent—Canadian, British, Japanese, don't matter; he can sound just like them. Like, he'll walk around the mall pretending he's from Australia: *just 'ere on 'oliday*. Girls eat it up 'cause he's really good-looking. They'll start following us around just to hear him say stuff. The only thing is, you never know about Derek. His moods can change faster than the weather. One second you're having a blast and laughing with him; the next, he's that person you're afraid of. I mean, one time he might be telling that Japanese guy with the plate of chicken samples in the food court, *That's nice of you, mate—be glad to give it a go*; the next time, *Eat your own dog meat, buddy*. That's why I'm hoping he'll be in one of his good moods when I get to his *new home* in New Jersey. Gramp says we're lucky Derek didn't get packed off to Florida like some of those other Maine kids like him *who no one gives a hoot about*. But ask me, Florida don't seem any farther away than New Jersey when you can't see him, and at least there, it don't snow at all.

The bus driver shuts off the overhead light, sucks the door shut, then waits for the traffic on Saint John Street to clear so he can pull out. Overhead reading lights start flicking on, and Gramp's is one of them. I leave mine off, rest my forehead against the cold window so I can see past my reflection and watch Burger King and the Dollar Store and Goodwill disappear.

The only thing I asked for for Christmas was to go see Derek. Told my parents it was the only thing I wanted. Even though for the past three years he's pretty much wrecked every holiday for our family, thinking of him being away from us at Christmas just tore me up. Couldn't sleep at night thinking about it. It's been bugging me since Thanksgiving, which was the first time since probably fourth grade we were able to have a meal like that without something bad happening. It was awesome having a day we didn't have to worry about things getting ruined, but it bummed me out not having him there. Made me feel guilty a part of me was glad he wasn't, that it was just me and Dad at the football game together and that the meal Ma always works so hard to make wasn't wrecked by one of his fights or trips to the ER.

"You comfortable?" Gramp wants to know.

"Doing good," I tell him. "What about you, Gramp?"

"Just glad I'm not the one having to do the driving."

Me too, 'cause Gramp's a lousy driver. He can't get across P-town without running a few lights or hitting something. When you get in his car, best thing to do is shut your eyes and start praying you'll see tomorrow. Even though he's her father, no way Ma would let me go see Derek if Gramp was behind the wheel. That's why she bought the bus tickets for me for Christmas. Truth is, I didn't see that one coming; didn't expect I'd be going with Gramp or going on a bus. Just figured Dad would drive—that me and Ma and him would go as a family. Even had it in my head we'd spend a night at some hotel with a pool 'cause, back in the day, before Derek started wigging out, we used to do stuff like that. Figured I'd get to go swimming, maybe go out for supper, definitely watch cable TV, for that's history now we live at Gramp's. So much for that stupid dream. Still, watching the black water and the lights of Casco Bay roll by, I tell Gramp, "Wish Ma and Dad coulda come."

"They would have if they could have," says Gramp.

I know he's right. My dad missed a lot a work on account

of Derek. Almost lost his job. Probably would've, too, if people he works with at JC Electric didn't donate him some of their vacation time. And Ma, who had to quit her job at Kohl's to stay home with Derek so he wouldn't hurt himself or burn down the house, just got hired temporary at L. L. Bean. She's been working all the hours she can get, hoping they'll keep her on after the holidays are over 'cause we're hurtin' for money.

"Things are really tight for them right now," says Gramp, like he's reading my mind instead of the newspaper. "Your father needs all the overtime he can get."

My dad still works full time at JC, but what Gramp means are all the under-the-table jobs he does at night doing wiring for relatives and people he knows. Nowadays, he's gone from six in the morning to sometimes midnight, so I hardly see him. So far this year he's only gotten to one of my basketball games. Thing is, I know it bothers him more than it does me. I keep telling him, *Don't worry 'bout it; it's just junior high— it's no big deal.* I seriously mean it, for I know he's working as hard as he can so we can buy another house and not have to live at Gramp's anymore. I love Gramp, but living with him sucks. His TV's so old it don't have a flat screen, and you can only get three channels 'cause he won't pay for cable, says it's *highway robbery.* Eight, six, thirteen, that's it.

I don't even have a bedroom, sleep in the den on a pull-out couch, and that's some comfortable. Have to lay just right or you'll get a spring in your back. And Gramp hates it if we move or touch any of his stuff 'cause it's been the same way since Gram died of cancer seven years ago. When Ma cleaned and changed the kitchen around, he just about had a heart attack. I thought she did a nice job, but he's still complaining how he *can't find a damn thing*. Then there's the bathroom; there's only one, and he's usually using it. The worst is in the morning, that's why I get up early so I can get in and outta there before he does his *morning constitutional*. That's what he calls it. Goes in there with a cigar and the newspaper and don't come out for half an hour. No joke, rather go in the bushes in the backyard than walk in that room after he's done. They'll have to evacuate this bus if he has a *constitutional* in that little box back there.

No way I'm gonna use it. We got transfers in Boston, New York, and Philadelphia—I'll go then. Gramp won't be able to wait, though—he'll be lucky if he makes it to Biddeford. He's got prostate problems, so he has to pee a lot. I stop watching the traffic on the turnpike to look at him. He has his head back, already starting to nod off. Gramp can sleep anywhere, even at the dentist getting his teeth cleaned. Kid you not; that really happened.

With him leaning back, I can see the girl in the seat across the aisle. She has short purple hair, black lips, earrings everywhere—nose, eyebrow, five at least in the ear I can see. She's wearing a leather jacket and earphones around her neck and reading a magazine. Back at the station she was chatting it up on her cell, sitting on a suitcase by the fake tree with blinkin' lights. Noticed her as soon as me and Gramp walked in. Definitely ghetto-goth but she has a great profile. I'd like to try those cheekbones. Brought my stuff but wouldn't want her to catch me. If I really concentrate, I can memorize her, do it later. Drawing for me's like music for Derek—something we can't live without. He loves the ancient metal—Led Zeppelin, Black Sabbath, Deep Purple, Def Leppard, bands like that. He knows all the names, all the lyrics. He used to play drums; now his set's out in Gramp's garage with all the other crap we own.

The girl musta felt me staring. She looks over and I melt back in my seat. I'm not like Derek when it comes to girls. No joke, he'd sit right down beside her and start talking like he'd known her his whole life. He'd find out all about her, too—where she was from, where she was going, why she's on the bus by herself. Wouldn't matter if she has a boyfriend, by the time we got to Old Orchard, which is the next exit, she'd be in love with him.

I'm serious: I've seen him in action. He always knows what girls wanna hear. He's got more mojo than Austin Powers—by the time he was my age, he'd already done it.

Me? I haven't even kissed a girl yet.

Closest I've come was walking Coleen Walsh home last fall. It was after a Friday night Portland–Cheverus football game, and I was stressin' out—had the hots for her since sixth-grade math class. Whole time we were walking Cumberland Avenue, she did all the talking 'cause I couldn't think about nothin' but finding out what those pouty lips I'd drawn a zillion times were finally gonna feel like against mine. Just about had a hard-on by the time we got to her house. But that was history soon as I saw her older brother, Joel, and his friends. They were sitting on the front steps drinking beers wrapped in paper bags, Jimmy Taylor wanting to know right off, with a butt hanging on his lips, "Ain't you Derek Andersen's brother?"

I tried to act cool for it ain't my neighborhood, and all those guys from the Hill are tough, so I looked right at him, said, "What about it?"

He started laughing, which grinds my gears 'cause I'm real touchy when it comes to Derek; plus there was no way I could kiss Coleen now, walked clear across town for nothing. Before I even had a chance to think, which, looking back, coulda gotten my teeth kicked in for sure, I asked him, "You got a problem with that?"

All three started laughing then, and Bangor, whose real name I don't even know but who's a definite tool, said, "Sounds just like 'im."

"Your brother's one crazy mutha," said Jimmy. "Funniest dude I know. Can charm a bum outta their last penny. What's he upta? Haven't seen him 'round."

That sorta changed things. I mean, I was some glad they seemed to like Derek. Meant I'd get to walk home without blood on my new hoodie I'd just bought at Goodwill, but what was I supposed to say? Yeah, he's so crazy he's in a mental hospital in New Jersey? That's not something I want people to know. I need to protect Derek's reputation while he's in there getting his brain straightened out. So I told Jimmy the same thing I tell anyone else that asks: "He's living in New Jersey working construction for my uncle."

Gramp buck-snorts loud enough to wake himself up.

"You okay, Gramp?" I ask, noticing the girl's looking our way, her brown eyes asking, *What the deuce?*

"Just needed to rest my eyes a minute," says Gramp.

"I'll shut your light off for you," I tell him, knowing it'll make it harder for her to see me. If that noise scared her, wait till the broccoli Gramp had at lunch catches up with him.

That's the thing about old people, they're not afraid to fart in public. If Gramp's gotta let one rip, he just does it, acts like it's no bigger deal than a cough or a sneeze, and for Gramp, eating broccoli's twice as deadly as B&M beans. *Better hold your breath and put your headphones on,* I want to warn her—gonna be a long ride.

CHAPTER 2

The girl goes back to her magazine. Gramp goes back to sleep. I go back to the window. It's starting to snow; I can see it in the headlights across the median. On a school night, I'd be praying for a blizzard, hoping when I woke up Kevin Mannix on *Storm Center* would be wearing his sweater and saying, *No school in Portland.* I love snow days, but it rots making them up. One year we didn't get outta school till almost July. Least I didn't. Derek got to the second week in June, said, *Screw this,* and just stopped going. If it'd been me, Dad would have dragged me out of bed and kicked my butt all the way down to King Junior. But Derek's Derek; he gets away with everything.

That's how it's always been. Even before he wigged for real, they always made excuses for him. That time it was *we think he might have mono*. As if! Soon as they left for work, he was out the door and on his way to East End Beach with Howie Bowman. Poor Howie used to get blamed for everything in our house 'cause he was from a *broken home* and was a *bad influence* on Derek. Ask me—and probably Howie's mother—it was the other way around. See, I know how Derek can be, how he can talk you into things, how he can make you believe what he's saying's true even when you know it isn't. No joke, they had a class in lying, he'd get an A plus in it. Thing is, I think he really believes some of the stuff he says 'cause he's practiced it so much, like, when any of the relatives ask him what he wants to do after high school, he'll say, *I'm going to be a merchant marine*. Then he'll tell them how he's already looking into it, how he plans on going to the academy up in Castine. He's never even been in a rowboat far as I know, but to listen to him talk, you'd think he'd already driven the CAT Ferry up to Nova Scotia.

"Goddamn snow," someone swears.

The crusty bum with the wicked bad BO is my guess. Kept getting whiffs of that nasty smell back at the station but wasn't sure who it was coming from till I walked in the men's room and saw him at the sink pouring wine into his Dunkin'

Donuts cup. *Do the world a favor, buddy, use some of that free soap on those lethal weapons!* That's what Derek woulda told him; wouldn't even be worried the guy might whack him in the head with that wine bottle. And knowing Derek, the guy would probably thank him. Me, I got outta there as fast as I could so I could breathe again. Just glad BO chose a seat in the back of the bus, is all I'm saying.

Other than him swearing about the snow, the bus is quiet enough to hear the sound of the wheels and the *click-clack*ing, super-sized windshield wipers. Everyone's sleeping or reading, or, like me, watching road signs: CHECK BRAKES (yellow/black letters), REDUCE SPEED (white/black letters), EMERGENCY CALL 911 (blue/white letters). After the sign LAST SERVICES ON TURNPIKE, I think up a better one as we roll by the Kennebunk Service Plaza: GET YOUR GAS AND GRAB A WHOPPER WHILE YOU STILL CAN. And when I spot MAINE/WORTH A VISIT/WORTH A LIFETIME (brown/white letters) I think, *Not!*

Our first stop's a dinky bus station in Wells. No one gets off, but a woman gets on with a crying baby and two little boys. While the driver's outside loading their luggage and their mother's trying to work her way up the steps with a screaming baby and a diaper bag the size of a suitcase, the two boys take off like rockets down the aisle, yelling to each other, "There's a seat! There's a seat! There's a seat!"

They pass us going 'bout forty, the shuffle and *clomp, clomp, clomp* of their snow boots loud enough to wake up Gramp. "What the heck was that?" he asks.

"Just some people gettin' on, Gramp."

"Where are we?"

"Wells."

He leans over and looks out the window. "Snowing."

"Started a little while ago."

"Coming down pretty good."

"Leo! Joey! Get back here! I need some help with the bag," says their mother, who then starts apologizing like crazy as she moves sideways down the aisle, her bag and humongo body bumping against people and seats. "Sorry, excuse me. Sorry, excuse me. Excuse me, sorry," the squirming, bawling baby in her arms making things even harder for her. "Earache," she informs us in a voice that sounds like she's gonna start bawling, too.

The girl with the purple hair jumps up, and next thing you know, she's hauling that lady's bag back to her own seat, telling her, "You can sit here; there's two seats. I'll find a place up back."

I'm thinking that was really nice of her. Then I realize—that lady and her screaming kid's gonna be sitting right next to us!

"Thank you so much," the mother tells Purplehead. "I really 'preciate it."

Staring at the baby—snot and tears running down its red face, howling like its finger's jammed in a car door—I wanna say, *Yuh, thanks a lot, Purplehead!*

But I don't got the stones to do that, so I look for another way out, tell Gramp, "I think we should move, too; that way, her other kids can be with her."

Soon as I make that suggestion, we hear the bathroom door slam shut and one of the boys yell, "Sorry, lady—didn't know you was in there."

"Good idea," says Gramp. "Let's move." He tells the woman what the plan is, and she keeps thanking us as we grab our stuff—Gramp his coat, newspaper, thermos full of coffee; me, my backpack and Mountain Dew. We head toward the back, but there ain't any places with two empty seats together, and after one of those little rug rats almost knocks Gramp over trying to get back down the aisle to his mom, Gramp grabs the first empty seat there is. "I'll be sitting right here, Zach, if you need anything."

Didn't know there were that many people on the bus till I start looking for a new seat. No way I'm gonna sit next to BO or the hit-and-run luggage lady who's taking up two seats like she's on a campout with her pillow and blanket and industrial-sized box of Cheez-Its. I consider the guy with the beard, but he's pretending he's asleep so he won't hafta have company, won't hafta move his coat and all his junk riding shotgun in the seat beside him—there's a winner for the Tool Award.

In panic mode, I look toward the front. Is it against the law to sit in the RESERVED FOR THE DISABLED seats if no one's in them? Figure probably—if it's against the law to step over a white line.

I'm thinking, *Where the hell am I gonna sit?* when the bus driver, who's already back behind the wheel, shuts off the lights and drowns out the baby's crying with "Next stop's Portsmouth!" He doesn't waste any time putting the bus in gear, and I almost take a digger when it starts hiccuping across the parking lot, making me wanna yell, *Move your Cheez-Its so I can sit down—will yuh, lady?*

"You can sit here."

Although the lights are off, I know who's making the offer. I don't have any other choice—though standing in the aisle all the way to Portsmouth does cross my mind. I fall into the seat beside her. "Thanks."

"No problem," says Purplehead. "That was really nice of you to move so those kids could sit there."

If you hadn't, I wouldn't have had to—that's the first thing that pops into my peanut brain, but I don't say a thing 'cause she smells a million times better than Gramp. I lose my hat so she won't think I'm a dork, shove it inside my pack.

"You'd think those jerks up front would've moved for her. I can't stand people like that. They see someone who needs help and just look the other way—know what I mean?"

I know what she means. I'm one of them. But I don't want her to know, so I say, "Yeah, I hate people like that."

I put my backpack down near my feet; it's either there or in the aisle, and I don't want anyone tripping over it on their way to the bathroom—got my sketchbook in there, don't want it getting wrecked. Thinking of my sketchbook makes me remember her cheekbones, and suddenly I'm wishing she'd turn on her light so I can study them up close, but you can't tell someone you just met, "I'd really like to draw your face." They'd tell yuh to find another seat.

"Where are you going?" she asks.

"New Jersey. You?"

"New York. My dad got transferred down there with his job. We were supposed to sell our house and move with him, but my parents got divorced instead."

Like, what am I supposed to say to that? I'm sorry? Tell her the truth? Selling your house really sucks, be glad you didn't have to? I'm not sure, so I take a sip of my warm Mountain Dew 'cause my mouth's drier than a host on Sunday.

"He's got a new wife and a baby now, so he couldn't make it up for Christmas. Should have just told him to send my presents in the mail like my sisters did, but..."

Purplehead doesn't finish, and that *but* starts to bug me as much as that baby who won't stop crying. "But what?"

"Wanted to see him, you know? Been a long time."

I know what she's saying—been a long time since I seen Derek, almost seven months. The day they came and took him, he put up a heck of a fight: put his fist right through the wall and the TV through the living room window. Took three big guys and a shot of something to finally get him in that jacket—and where was I when he was hollering for me to help? Hiding in the bathroom with the door locked, that's where.

"Have Kleenex, will travel." She blows her nose, sniffs back the tears. "Sorry," she says. "I don't even know you. You're going to think I'm a nutbag."

"No I don't," I tell her, 'cause thinking about the last time I saw Derek makes me misty, too. See, I couldn't stay in the bathroom, couldn't stand listening to Ma out there crying and Dad yelling, *Don't hurt him! Don't hurt him!* Come out just in time to see them wheeling Derek out the front door, him strapped to the stretcher with black belts, his head the only thing able to move, his mouth looking like bloody Cool Whip as he screamed at me, *I'll friggin' kill you!*

"Think after two years I'd be over it," she tells me, "but sometimes it still gets to me, you know? Like when I see a mom like that with little kids and no one to help her. Been there, done that, got the T-shirt: My Dad Sucks, What About Yours?" She starts laughing. "I don't believe I just unloaded that on you."

I like her laugh. It sounds real. Not that giggle crap most girls do. "It's okay," I tell her. "You'll never see me again, so who cares?"

She laughs even louder, then reaches up and snaps on the light. "How old are you?"

As she checks me out with those brown eyes that are so beautiful she don't need the makeup, I think of telling her I'm in high school. I clear my throat 'cause, even though my voice changed last summer, it still cracks on me sometimes. "I'll be fourteen in June," I say, and it surprises me I told her the truth when I hadn't planned on it.

"You seem a lot older than that." She leans back in her seat and tilts her face toward the light, says, "Too bad."

Too bad? "What's that mean?"

"I'm a sophomore."

I get her now: I know the law—high school kids never go out with anyone in junior high. "No problem," I tell her. "You're not my type."

That cracks her up. "So what's your type?" she wants to know, like I'm a joke.

Feel like telling her, *Someone who doesn't wear a hunk of metal in their eyebrow.* "What's it to you?"

"Just curious."

I look away, knowing my face is turning red, can feel it burning. I hate how it does that, how it lets people know I'm embarrassed or mad or trying to lie. "The baby stopped crying," I say to change the subject.

But she won't let it go. "C'mon," she says. "If you tell me, I'll tell you."

That seems fair, but, "You go first."

She gives me this grin, then leans over with a hand covering those black lips and whispers, "Bad boys."

I jump back like she just gave me a carpet shock. "What?"

"You know," she says. "The good looking, tough, not afraid of anyone kind, that don't care what other people think."

I'm thinking, *You'd really love Derek, then.*

"Your turn."

"Long blond hair. Blue-gray eyes." Coleen Walsh.

But her brother Joel's gonna make sure that never happens.

25

Ever since I walked Coleen home that night, she's been keeping her distance. *Hi, how you doing?* That's all I get. Probably told her to stay the heck away from me after hearing those stories Jimmy and Bangor told about Derek.

"That's it?" asks Purplehead.

"Smart," I tell her. "The kinda girl you'd walk all the way across town for."

"Mmm," she says, as if she just tasted a Tony's doughnut. "I like that. Someone you'd walk all the way across town for."

"Even when it's wicked cold out," I add.

"I don't know any guys I'd do that for."

"No boyfriend?"

"At my high school? News flash—I'm not what you'd call mainstream material."

I laugh; know exactly what she means. Ma would have a cow if I brought home a girl with hair like hers. Still, seeing her up close, that tiny diamond in her nose looks kinda pretty. I figure if she lost the ring in the eyebrow and the makeup, and put a hat on, she'd really be hot.

"Put it this way," she says, "no one in hicksville's got my cell number."

"Where's that?"

"Searsmont."

"Never heard of it."

"Exactly."

"So there's no bad boys there?"

"Oh, there's a couple; just none I'd walk across town for, even on a nice day."

I see the oldest of the two kids, who looks about five, coming down the aisle holding on to his crotch, and I know where he's headed. The motion of the bus makes him walk like a drunk, and when he almost lands in my lap, I reach out to steady him, say, "Careful there, little buddy. Don't hurt yourself."

"T'anks," he tells me, and keeps on going.

"What a cutie," says Purplehead. "Maybe having a little brother won't be so bad."

I could fill her in on what it's like to be the little brother. Name for that blog be *Overrated*. I'll tell yuh, with Derek it's no cakewalk. He has to be the center of attention 24/7, no matter what mood he's in. You never get to sit up front with a brother like that; back seat is where you're always riding 'cause there's no way yuh gonna win. Don't matter what it is—what we're gonna eat, where we're gonna go, what we're gonna watch on TV—just easier on the whole fam to let him have his way, let him run the show, 'cause he'll just wear you down and it ain't worth the fight.

"You have any brothers or sisters?" she asks.

"No sisters, just a brother."

"Older or younger?"

"He's seventeen."

She raises her eyebrows, teases me with a look. "He as cute as you?"

Cute's the word I always get stuck with. Derek gets *handsome* from all the relatives, *hottie* from all the girls. He's always bragging, *I can't help it if I'm God's gift to women,* and everyone always laughs when he says it 'cause it's true. When my parents tried that tough love route and kicked him outta the house and he was living in the garage, you never knew who was gonna walk outta there on a Sunday morning. Be at the kitchen sink getting a drink of water, there'd go some babe through our backyard with a hand trying to hide her face.

"He got the looks in the family," I tell her.

"You didn't do so bad," she says, and that makes me feel good 'cause, hey, you know? She's in high school—no reason for her to lie to a dipwad in eighth grade.

"Would you like to see some pictures of my little sisters?"

"Sure," I tell her, and while she's digging through her bag with the skulls on it, we hear this: "Help, Momma! Help!"

I look down the aisle toward the bathroom. Now the kid's screaming, "I'm gonna fall in!"

Everyone starts laughing 'cept Purplehead, who stabs my ribs with an elbow. "Go help him!"

Me? Why not one of those grown-ups—say, that lady shovelin' down the Cheez-Its; she's closer. But it's clear not one of those adults is getting up. Ain't their kid, not their problem.

Queen Help Everybody jabs me again, says, "Hurry up," and off I go, wishing I never met her, and thinking, *What am I supposed to do?*

Walking on a bus going seventy ain't easy. Gotta zigzag my way down there—time I knock on the door, I'm sweating like a pig. "You okay, little buddy?"

"Help!" he says.

Not sure if it's my luck or his, but the door's not locked.

I swing it open, and there he is, wedged in the pot, his short little legs straight up in the air, his arms hanging on to the seat for dear life. Sue me for laughing, but he looks wicked funny.

"Hang on," I tell him, and as I lift him off the toilet and lower his feet to the floor, he tells me how it happened. "I was tryin' ta wipe."

The kid's killing me, gotta chew my lip so I don't crack up.

"Keep da door shut," he orders. "Don't want no one see my willy."

There's not enough room in there for the two of us to fart, but I tell him, "Don't worry, I won't open it till yuh ready." And as he hauls up his Spider-Man skivvies and the pants swimming down around his boots, I'm some glad for him that it's me in here, not that Cheez-It lady.

"T'anks," he says, then barges by me and out the door, leaving me to flush the toilet. Leaving me there wondering— where's that stuff go?

CHAPTER 3

I'm hardly back in my seat a second before the kid shows up, dragging his little brother by the hand, who can't be more than three but has a head the size of a watermelon.

"What?" I ask. "He got to go, too?"

The older boy shakes his head no, says, "He still wears Pampas, stupid."

Should tell him, *That's a real nice thing to call someone who just saved your little butt.* Instead, I ask, "How'd you know my name's Stupid?"

The older one gets it, but the younger one doesn't laugh till he sees his big brother bust up.

Queen Help Everybody leans across my lap, and while she

asks them, "What's your names?" I catch a whiff of her leather coat and something else nice. Maybe oranges?

"I'm Leo," says the older boy. "He's Joey."

Beneath the leather coat and her sweater and her bra, I can feel her left breast pressing against the back of my hand, and I'm hoping she's gonna talk to these kids all the way to New York.

But that dream's over with the very next question. "Clown?" Joey asks, pointing at her.

Purplehead sits up and starts laughing. "Don't you love kids?" she asks me. "They're not inhibited at all."

Inhibited? Don't even gotta guess what that means, but I notice Leo don't like her laughin' at his little brother.

"If you ain't a clown," he says, "why you got purple hair for and that black stuff on your lips?"

Now, that's what I love about little kids, they take one look at a person and tell yuh how it is.

"Because I like being different," says Purplehead in a voice that sounds like a teacher. "I don't want to be like everyone else."

I watch Leo chew on that for a nanosecond. "Yeah," he agrees, "wish we could have Halloween every day. I was Spida-Man this year. Momma bought my costume at Walmart. It cost big bucks."

The word *Halloween* must've triggered something inside

that huge head of Joey's 'cause his eyes light up like a slot machine hittin' the muthaload. He pushes by Leo, shoves out his grubby little hand, demands, "Treat!"

Not to be outdone by his little brother, Leo jumps into the action. "Trick or treat, smell my feet; give me something good to eat!"

Knowing the hand he's waving in front of my face wasn't washed back there in that bathroom, I push it away. These little rug rats are starting to bug me. No way I'm gonna give 'em any of the food Ma packed for me and Gramp. They get a taste of her chocolate chip cookies, they'll be back quicker than pigeons in a McDonald's parking lot.

"I have some apples," Purplehead tells them. "Would you like one?"

Leo cuts right to the chase. "Got any candy?"

Joey comes alive again. "Cannybar!" he shouts and worms his way closer, till he's hugging my knees and stepping on my backpack.

"Easy!" I tell him, 'cause those boots of his are probably wrecking my sketchpad and the vintage issue of *X-Men* my best bud, Frankie Altman, lent me. Probably crushing Ma's cookies and turning the ham sandwiches into pancakes, too. "Let me move my backpack, big guy."

So there I am, sideways in my seat and bent over down

there like rubber man trying to rescue my stuff from beneath those stomping feet when I catch another whiff, but it don't smell like leather or oranges—Joey's packin' a load in those Pampers. I grab my backpack and come up for air, and now she's asking them, "What about some carrots?"

"No way," says Leo, and I'm thinking the same thing. I mean, what kid wants carrots?

"How about some chocolate chip cookies?" I ask them, for I don't care anymore—I just want the little one off my leg and both of them outta my face.

"Cookie!" screams Joey.

"You should probably ask their mother if that's okay," Purplehead informs me.

"Why? You were gonna give 'em apples."

"Duh," she says. "Something healthy."

"We can have cookies," says Leo. "Momma don't care long as we don't bug her, right, Joey?"

Joey nods, and it makes me think of a line from a movie I saw: *His head's so huge, it's got its own weather system.*

Then the bus driver comes over the mic. "Boys, you need to go back to your seats. No playing in the aisle; don't want anyone getting hurt."

"Hurry," says Leo. "Me and Joey gotta go, or he'll kick us off the bus and make us walk."

"No he won't," says Purplehead.

"Ah-huh," says Leo. "That's what Momma said if we ain't good."

I hand them over the loot—two cookies each.

"T'anks," says Leo, then asks his little brother, "Want me carry yours, Joey, so you don't fall and break-id them?"

"No!" says Joey. "Mine!"

"Okay. You drop yours, you can't have mine," says Leo, and Joey seems to know what that means 'cause he gives 'em up.

"Hold on my shirt," orders Leo, and off they go, Joey latched on to the back of his brother's Portland Pirates sweat-shirt, Leo leading the way like an airplane in rough weather, his outstretched arms giving him balance while holding two cookies in each hand.

I lean out into the aisle to watch; make sure they get back all right.

"They okay?" asks Purplehead.

"Yeah," I tell her, and sitting back in my seat, I get the urge to draw what I'd just seen. I take out my sketchbook. Find a clean page. Go to work.

When we were little, Derek always watched out for me. Like Leo, he would've told me to hang on to him—mighta taken a bite out of one of my cookies, but he'd make sure I got back to my seat safe. And like Joey, I would've trusted him, woulda handed over the loot in a heartbeat.

In them, I saw us. Derek, the one always in charge: the

one who showed me how to escape from my crib, how to pedal my Big Wheel, how to pee in the bushes so we didn't waste time going inside. When I think back to their age, his is the only face I see clearly. It was his bed I crawled into after a bad dream, him I ran to if kids picked on me, him I jumped off the top of the slide for. That history makes me wanna draw those brothers: Leo leading the way, Joey hanging on. Makes me wanna go back there to when we were young and life was good.

"Sweet," says Purplehead. "Wish I could draw."

"Shh," I tell her. I don't wanna talk, don't wanna stop, the caricature just a skeleton of the picture inside my head. I leave her and the bus, go to the zone, to the only place where I can make sense of things that don't. Like, why I feel so jealous of the two little rug rats I just met.

Wasn't till junior high that Derek started changing. It was like one day he was Derek, the next, some kid I didn't even know or want to. My parents said it was normal, said my dad had been a little wild at that age, too, so they made up excuses for him. *Boys will be boys; he's turning into a teenager; junior high's such a rough stage.* They blamed the way he started dressing on *peer pressure*, his bad grades on *teachers who couldn't teach*, blamed his quitting basketball on *playing time* and 'cause *the coach didn't like him.* But from the back seat I saw it another way: *he's turning into a real tool; you let him get away with everything.* But they wouldn't listen to me, didn't want me sayin' *he's a headcase*, didn't want to hear the truth: *he needs help.* Told me, *Keep out of it, Zach. This doesn't concern you! You're only making things worse! We have enough to deal with right now!* Got that grief so many times, I gave up and hung out at Frankie Altman's as much as I could.

It feels good to crank out the picture: the boys animated, exaggerated, those cookies big as plates, the trip back to their seat a thousand times more dangerous, the inside of the bus magnified and tilted, the Cheez-It lady shooting them a look with bullet eyes. If Derek were here, he'd get it—whenever he brags about me, he tells people, *Zach's a comedian with a pencil.*

But Derek can never leave it there. He has to make 'em laugh, has to tell them, *Zach used to take the poop out of his diapers and draw pictures on our bedroom wall.* And after they're done laughing at me for that, he always adds, *That's why he's such a good bullshit artist.*

Can't tell you if that story of his really happened, but I do know I like stretching the truth, like making fun of it—Joey's head's so huge it takes up the whole aisle.

CHAPTER 4

When I finish the rough sketch and remember where I am, the Greyhound's already cruisin' over the big, steel bridge in Portsmouth, New Hampshire. I hold up the work to study it from a distance, and Purplehead's right there, hanging over my shoulder with her Tic Tac breath tickling my ear. "Whaddaya think?"

"I'd hate to see the way you'd draw me," she answers.

I wasn't expecting that—I was figuring on a little glory, you know, like *that's awesome* or *you're wicked good*. Feels like she just kicked me in the stones.

"You're cruel," I tell her.

"Look who's talking."

"What?"

"Duh! Just don't show it to their mother," she says. "She might not think it's funny."

I flip the book shut, shove it in my pack. I don't give a flying fart what Purplehead thinks. Who is she, anyway? People like her slay me. Act like they're right up there with Jesus, as if they don't think the same things—tell me no one else on this bus noticed the noggin on that kid. Has a cranium big enough to get him into Ripley's Believe It or Not, and she thinks the WIDE LOAD sign I drew on the back of his head's not funny?

Like Derek says, *Screw 'em if they can't take a joke.* Hey, if she can't take that one, no way can she handle the other sketches I got in there. Like the one of Dad pounding on the bathroom door, Derek on the other side, sitting on the black-and-white diamond floor, X-Acto knife floatin' in a river of blood, thought cloud above his head reading, *Can't anyone get any privacy in this house?*

She'd probably think I was a sicko, and maybe I am, but when you live in my house, you gotta have a wicked sense of humor, or you're fishbait.

"This is them," she says, holding out the photo she'd been looking for earlier. "That's Jordon, she's ten; Lindsey's seven."

Even though she just dissed my work, I'm curious. I take the picture from her. The two girls staring back at me have long hair and new everything—clothes, backpacks, sneakers. Definitely one of those first-day-back-to-school pictures where your mother makes you stand on the porch and smile wearing all the new stuff she bought yuh. Ma made us do it every year till this one. So what's that say? I wonder. 'Cause Derek wasn't there, a picture of just me ain't good enough?

"Jordon's a walking Wikipedia," says Purplehead. "She wants to be a veterinarian. And Lindsey's the little fashion queen. If I have to dress up for something, I have her pick out my clothes."

There's definitely a family resemblance—same high cheekbones, a younger version of her. "Is that what your hair used to look like?" I ask, 'cause if it was, seriously, she should have left it alone.

Reaching up to comb her fingers through what's left and now purple, she says, "Don't you like it?"

I like her sisters' better—waist length, the shade of brown that gets streaks of blond in the summer. Got a feeling she don't wanna hear that, so I tell her, "Yuh stylin'—look like Marvel Girl."

"Marvel Girl?"

"You know, from X-Men? The comic series?" It's my favorite, not only 'cause of the awesome penciling, but 'cause I can relate to the story. I'm totally hooked. Thing is, though I get the right-and-wrong preaching of Professor Xavier and his crew of mutants, who are supposed to be the good guys and are always stepping in to save the human race, I can definitely relate to Magneto and his mutant gang, who everyone's supposed to hate.

"I'm not into those kinds of movies," says Purplehead.

I pull out the issue of *Tomorrow People* that Frankie scored at Comic Sense. He'd lent it to me to read on the ride, but I couldn't wait, had started it while sitting in that pit of a bus station where the only other things to read were the people and a sign on the wall—THIS IS A BIG COUNTRY. NOBODY COVERS IT LIKE GREYHOUND.

I hand her the copy, try to explain. "See, the mutants are these characters with special powers they discover when they're teenagers, like Bobby Drake, aka Iceman, who finds out he can freeze stuff. So you got the good mutants, who use their powers to help save the world, and the bad mutants, who use theirs to take over the world, and in the middle is the human race, who hate mutants no matter if they're good or bad."

That's why I can see where Magneto is coming from, 'cause if you're a mutant, you get screwed no matter if you're good or bad, but I don't bother to explain that, for I can tell by the way she's flipping through the pages that to her it's just a comic book and nothing else.

Still, I can't stop from trying to let her know that it's so much more. "It's like there's all these parallels to today's society and politics and—"

She stops me before I can finish; all she cares about is "Which one's me?"

I lean a little closer, check out the page she's on. "Keep going," I tell her. "There's a wicked good picture of her comin' up." And when Purplehead finds it, she starts laughing.

I stare down at Marvel Girl, whose sexy green eyes are looking right back at me, but in the story are really looking at that schmo of a cop who's got Storm locked up in his jail. It's an awesome picture—her leaning on his desk, those beautiful boobs just about bursting outta her black leather top as she uses her special power to fog his mind, make him believe she's some guy from the FBI. Once I had a dream that Marvel Girl and me were down at Deering Oaks. It was one of those really real dreams, you know, the kind in color, the kind you remember details about when yuh wake up. Like how we were standing on the stone bridge and there were people walking by with tennis rackets; how she kept saying, "Don't worry," 'cause she could just fog their minds so they wouldn't know what we were doing. It was a great dream till I woke up and had to hide the evidence.

"The hair's kinda the same," admits Purplehead. "But I'll never have a body like that in this lifetime."

If she did, I'd be wanting to draw more than her cheek-bones.

"And who'd want to?" she asks. "She looks like an anorexic on steroids."

"No way!" I tell her. "You blind?"

"Then they wonder why half the girls in this country have eating disorders. I mean, come on, they shove that garbage down our throat everyplace we look from the time we're born. Brainwash us . . ."

Whenever Ma's ticked off, Gramp likes to say *she's got a bee in her bonnet,* and though I'm not sure what Purplehead's yapping about, she's definitely got a bee in hers. She starts talking so fast it's like hearing a different language, like being in Mrs. Tibbits's English class while she's dissecting a story, and you're sittin' there wondering, Did I read the right one?

". . . with commercials and movies and every magazine ad we see . . ."

No joke, doing book reports for her was a nightmare. Used to kill me—Mrs. Tibbits and her *author's intentions.* She never let you get away with just saying what the stupid story was about.

". . . make us think we'll only look good in their skinny jeans if we're a size two, that we're not good enough unless we're built like a stick with silicone boobs . . ."

Way I figure it, writing's like drawing; half the time, things happen without you even thinking about it. Start drawing a line, and next thing you know, you got a picture, and while you were doing it, you weren't thinking about it at all.

"... it's everywhere—no fat, low fat, call Jenny Craig..."

But nooo. Every little thing had to mean something to Mrs. Tibbits. She totally ruined *Lord of the Flies* for me.

"... so it's no big surprise your hero there looks like she's never eaten a meal in her life and lives on exercise and plastic surgery.... Hey—are you even listening to me?"

I nod. Had heard enough to know she's jealous of Marvel Girl. Also remember hearing the word *fat* a couple of times, so I need to talk about something else. That's one of Derek's Ten Commandments—*If a girl starts talkin' 'bout being fat, change the subject el pronto.* "Wonder how long we'll stop here for?"

Purplehead looks out the window. "Why do they put bus stations in the worst parts of town?"

It's a good question. I think I might even know the answer—poor people take buses; rich people own cars and take planes. Makes sense, don't it? Put the bus station where the poor people can walk to it. I don't tell her that, though, in case I'm wrong. 'Sides, you never know, the bus station in her town could be right by her house, so I play it safe, say, "I know what yuh mean."

44

"It's really snowing now," she says as the overhead lights snap on and some people start to gather their stuff.

"Portsmouth," calls the driver, and I look down the aisle, trying to get a glimpse of Gramp. He's talking up a storm with some bald guy in the seat beside him. Though Gramp usually don't say much around the house, get him down to Hannaford, and he'll talk the ear off of anyone he runs into. Once we were in the meat section a whole hour getting his red hot dogs 'cause he was chatting it up with some old geeza he'd played football with. Gramp was a standout, three-sport athlete at PHS. Get what I'm saying? He runs into anyone who calls him Speeding Eddie, I go put the ice cream back.

While people are getting off, the oldest of the rug rats sneaks up the aisle to ask, "Got any more cookies? Me and Joey still hungry."

He's looking at me like one of those starvin' kids in the Food for the Poor flyers that come in our mail every month. How yuh say no to that? Ma can't; she's always sending them ten bucks when my dad ain't looking. "Sure," I tell him. "Hang on."

While I'm fishing for the cookies, Purplehead asks, "Do you like riding on the bus, Leo?"

He nods, then announces, "My house is all broke, so we going to Aunty's. She's gonna buy the pink stuff for Sister's ears so she won't cry."

"Oh," says Purplehead. "That's nice."

"Yeah, Aunty loves us. She makes good food. I like her house the best. But my dad can't go there. Aunty don't like him."

"Why?" asks Purplehead.

"He's mean when he drinks too much beers. He throwed a chair at me and punched my mom and made her face bleed. But don't tell no one. Don't want him to go to jail and never see him again."

The kid's story makes me wanna give him all the food I got, even the stuff Ma packed for Derek in the cooler riding with our suitcases in those bins under the bus. "Here," I tell him, forking over the ham sandwich I was gonna have for supper and what's left of the cookies and my bag of Doritos.

"Wowza! T'anks!" he says, like he just won the lotto. Then, checking out the sandwich through the Baggie, he wants to know, "Got any with no mustard? Joey don't like mustard."

"That's all I got," I lie. I can't give him the one that only has mayo—that's Gramp's. "Take it or leave it."

"I like mustard," he says real quick, like he's scared I might neg on the offer. "I eat anything, even gum on the sidewalk."

"Gum on the sidewalk?" says Purplehead, like she's trying to get a visual. "Sick."

Leo cocks his head at me, asks, "She your girlfriend?"

"Think your mother's calling yuh," I tell him, and he gets the hint. With a good grip on his haul, he makes tracks, and I watch him push and bump his way down the aisle through the line of passengers waiting to get off. Though he disappears from sight, I hear "Score! Look what I gotted for us, Joey!"

"Poor kid," says Purplehead. "Did you hear what he said about his father?"

I nod. *My house is all broke.* I can definitely relate to that. Derek on a tear, smashing everything—furniture, walls, windows—the anger in him so scary the best thing to do is run for cover, hide out in the bathroom where I can lock the door. How many hours did I waste in there waiting for him to calm down or for Ma or Dad to come home? No wonder that's where I went the day they were hauling him away— only safe place in the house.

Also know where that little kid's comin' from when he says, *Don't want him to go to jail and never see him again,* 'cause when Derek was fourteen he *borrowed* a car and spent a hundred and twenty-two days in juvie just waitin' for his case to be heard. Remember I was wicked scared something bad would happen to him in there, being locked up with all those older kids. But if anything did, he never talked about it. Only thing Derek said about that place were jokes. Like, *the reason it's called The Boys Training Center is 'cause it's training boys for Windham's prison*, or *if you think I got head problems, you should meet some of the friends I made in there*, or *I didn't miss one day of school*.

Outside the driver starts sliding suitcases out of the storage bin, and I can feel the rumble of it under my feet. The line grows shorter, and the blast of cold air coming up the aisle through the open door makes me wanna put my coat back on. I'm standing up to stretch my legs, when I hear BO yell, "That's right! No taxes in New Hampshire!" Then he tells the suitcase guy, who's on his way back from the bathroom, "Hey, Kung Foo, ask him to make a pit stop at that big liquor store, and I'll buy you a lottery ticket."

Suitcase hesitates for just a second, then tells him real politely, "Sorry, I don't speak English. And I never gamble."

It's perfect. The guy's a riot. Everyone gets the joke 'cept BO, so I sit back down before he tries to bribe me.

I lean over to look out the window, catch a view of the snow that's made the glass wet and blurry. It started out that thick kind with big flakes, but now it's the thin kind that blows and drifts and makes the streetlights look foggy.

Purplehead turns to look out, too, and I feel her feathery hair brush my cheek as she cups a hand against the window.

The closeness of her feels good, takes the edge off that awful feeling of Derek being gone. Don't matter how many months it's been, that's hard to live with; I can't get used to the quiet, or wakin' up and remembering why he ain't there. It kicks the crap outta me when I least expect it—hearing a song he likes, or a joke he'd get, or right now watching that snow and remembering how we used to make forts and go sliding down Camel Hill and jump up and down like idiots whenever channel six said, *No school in Portland*. That's what I'm thinking when I realize my chin's resting on Purplehead's shoulder. And suddenly I don't dare to breathe 'cause it feels so good having someone to share the storm with. But like anything good in my life, it don't last long.

"Would you like to sit by the window?" she asks in a way that says, *Hey, kid, you're invading my space*.

"Oh, sorry," I tell her, leaning back so quick I bump her nose.

"Ow," she moans.

Now I'm really sorry. "You okay?"

Still holding on to her nose, she starts laughing. "You're dangerous."

"Wrong brother."

"What?"

I hadn't meant to say that out loud. "Nada," I tell her, but she's not listening. She's scoping out the people starting to get on. Probably doing the math in that purple head of hers, hoping for some empty seats so I'll get lost. But we're both outta luck 'cause the line of people getting on is longer than the one that just got off.

A group of jocks lead the pack, two of them tall enough to have to duck their heads so they don't crack 'em on the ceiling. I'm betting they play B-ball for some high school, and, 'cause of the green face paint, that the Celtics are playin' in Boston. The four of them head right for the back, the second guy to pass me shoving the first one along with, "Keep moving."

"Shut up, Chappy," says the one that took the push. "Ain't my fault it's snowing. Next time ask your old man if we can use his BMW."

The line behind the jocks disappears as people snatch up the handful of open seats in the front, and suddenly there don't seem to be enough to go around. The last B-ball kid's standing in the aisle, looking like me about an hour ago. "Excuse me, ma'am, can I sit there?" he asks.

But Cheez-It ain't sharing her couch with no one. "I have phlebitis," she tells him. "I need to keep my legs elevated."

"Oh," he says, and by the look on his face, I know he's wondering the same thing I am: Can you catch that?

The driver's back on board and stomping the snow off his boots, the sound makin' everyone look in his direction. "Find a seat, son," he calls down to the kid, then he begins his speech, which, this being the third time I've heard it, ain't funny anymore. Finally, he kills the overhead lights, says, "Next stop's Newburyport."

"Then Boston?" someone asks.

"Then Boston," he answers.

Meanwhile, the Celtic fan has grabbed the only seat he could get—the empty one next to BO—poor schmuck. I was him, I'd be asking for my money back. No way I'd sit next to that air-pollutin' cootie carrier. He's the kinda scumbag Ma was talking about; bet he has a few live ones hopping on that head.

You should have seen BO in the bathroom back in Portland. Thought he was so clever, it's pathetic. Shut your eyes; I'll give you a visual. He's at the sink—standing sideways, back to me—and thinks I can't see what he's doing. Last detail—he's in front of a mirror. *Peek-a-boo! See the wine bottle, too!* Be what I caption that one.

Slays me how adults think if you're a kid, you're automatically stupid. Might be able to fool the bus driver, but I know what's packed in his Hannaford suitcase; I know what BO's drinking outta that Dunkin' Donuts cup. Ma drinks the same stuff on Thanksgiving, Christmas, and Easter. She cuts it with ginger ale, so one bottle lasts her a whole year. My dad teases her about it, calls it *Ma's Fruit of the Vine*. He only drinks beer. It's nothin' but Budweiser for him. Gramp, he likes rum, keeps a bottle of Captain Morgan on the top shelf in the pantry, has a shot after supper every night. And Derek, he drinks anything he can get his hands on. First time he came home wasted was the summer he was going into seventh grade. He'd made up a big story about Howie's uncle having a camp on Peaks Island, said they were gonna take the ferry down and stay overnight. Course that wasn't the plan at all. The real plan was to go to some kegger on the West End, then sleep out in Weasel's backyard. Problem was, Derek got so drunk, Weasel and Howie thought he was gonna die on 'em after he passed out. Somehow they managed to haul him home. Dad answers the door in his underwear, wondering who the hell's ringing our bell at one in the morning, and there's Derek laid out on the front lawn like Christ on the cross.

"What's with the green faces?" asks Purplehead.

I see Poor Schmuck shoot his buddies the finger so they know he's not happy about the seating arrangements, then I turn and look at Purplehead. "Must be goin' to a Celtics game."

"I hate jocks," she says, and though I got a feeling there's more to the story than that, I don't really care what it is. I reach up and shut my light off. Guess I won't be telling her I'm a basketball star.

CHAPTER 5

When I was four, Derek saved my life. Even if he didn't constantly remind me, it's somethin' I'd never forget. We were having a barbecue, and the Altmans, our next-door neighbors, were there with their tribe. That's what my dad always calls their kids. He likes to say the Altmans gave up birth control for Lent 'cause Frankie and his four brothers were all born in November. He always laughs when he says it, so I always knew it was a joke, but I never got it till last year's sex ed class.

Anyhow, our parents are on the deck, cooking, talking, drinkin' beers, and all us kids are chowing down at the picnic table, when Pat, who's Derek's age and a pro at burping, lets one roll. Everyone starts laughing, and I start choking on my hot dog.

I'm not sure what's the worst way to die. Andy Law thinks being sliced and diced with a chainsaw one limb at a time, and Frankie thinks getting doused with gasoline and then having someone put a match to yuh. But I think waking up in a coffin and realizing you've been buried alive has to be right up there. Seriously, having almost bit the dust suffocating, I can tell you not being able to breathe is horrible. Even to this day I can't stand anything around my neck—sends me into panic mode, and right back to that day in our backyard when, according to Ma, I turned *three shades of purple and was limper than a rag doll*. In her version: *It was a nightmare. By the time I flew off that deck, your brother was holding you upside down by the ankles and pumping you like a salt shaker.*

My dad's take on what happened ain't as dramatic: *I just thought you boys were horsing around till your mother started screaming like a banshee.*

Course, Derek's got a lot of versions, and in every one of them he's the hero, but the details depend on who he's telling the story to and what kinda mood he's in. If it's his friends, he usually starts out with *Our parents were so busy poundin' down the beers, they didn't even know what was happening,* and he'll supply all the gross stuff like how my eyes were popping outta my head and how I pissed my pants and how the Altmans' black Lab ate the piece of hot dog after it shot outta my mouth like a rocket.

With the relatives, he tones it down: *I just held him upside down by the ankles, and when I couldn't shake it outta him, I nailed him in the back with my knee, and it popped right out.* With them, he tries to act like it was no big deal, just the big brother doing what he has to. He knows if Ma's around, she'll jump right in and do the rest for him: *if it wasn't for Derek, we would have been going to a funeral the next day.*

But with me, Derek only uses the short versions. If he's mad at me, it's *I shoulda let you choke on that rot dog* or *next time I'll just sit there and watch.* And if he wants something from me, say, do his chores or lend him money or lie for him, it's *c'mon, you still owe me—weren't for me, you wouldn't even be alive.*

But there's something Derek never mentions in any of his versions: how he'd started bawling right in front of the whole Altman tribe when he realized I was all right. And even though I'm sick of hearing that hot dog story and sick of Derek holding it over me, his bawling that day's something I never mention, either. That's the way it is between us. Me and Derek never say that "love you" crap out loud, but it's there, yuh know? It's sorta like that little rug rat scouting out food for his brother and knowing he don't like mustard.

"Do you have any more gum?" Purplehead wants to know.

"Hang on," I tell her, then start feeling around for it, finally find it in the side pocket of my pack.

She snaps on her light so she can see and, looking down at the package of gum Gramp gave me for the ride, starts laughing. "Juicy Fruit?"

"Better than nothing," I point out.

She takes a piece and instead of thanks, tells me, "I should be home with a pint of Ben & Jerry's watching a Stephen King movie."

"Just look out the window," I tell her. "*Storm of the Century.*"

"*The Shining!*" she says. "Even better." Then in a low, scratchy voice, tells me, "Red rum, red rum."

I wiggle my index finger at her, say, "T o n y."

We laugh at that 'cause we're on the same page, and for a while we talk Stephen King movies. Blows me away how she knows all the lines—*Seven cents, Vern?*—and, like Derek, is wicked good at imitating voices—*Tommyknockers, Tommyknockers, knocking at the door.*

From there we move on to TV. Her favorite shows are ones I never watch—*Vampire Diaries* and *Bones.* She asks, "Isn't that a cartoon?" when I tell her mine's *Family Guy.*

She says TV and movies are her life, says she wants to go into film and video, says she's thinking of NYU, but there's some school in Chicago she likes even better.

"That's cool," I tell her, but I'm kinda wondering if what she's sayin's like Derek's big plan to be a merchant marine. I mean, how you really supposed to know what you wanna be at their age?

Or my age?

Or in first grade when teachers and grown-ups start asking that stupid question?

"What about you?" she asks.

I don't even have a good lie to give her. When yuh sleeping on a couch with bad springs and yuh family's falling apart, there's no looking ahead at things like that. Only future you got's gettin' by today and hoping you can scrounge up enough change in the junk drawer for hot lunch. "All I know's I wanna make a lotta money."

I see Gramp coming down the aisle, heading toward the can for the second time since we left Portland. By the way he's shuffling, I can tell his bad knee's hurtin', and the wet floor's slippery. Maybe it's the light, but he's looking wicked old to me—his walk, white hair, his shaky hand as he reaches out to grip the next seat—tears me right up.

Getting old really sucks. 'Specially when you used to look

like he did in that photo album I found in the den. Reminded me of Derek: same good looks, ultra jock build. Gotta be hard going from a football hero to an old fart who can barely get around. His doctor says Gramp needs to have his knee replaced, for his arthritis's so bad he's walkin' bone on bone, but Gramp says he ain't in enough pain yet to have that done, which is a load 'cause I hear him groaning in the middle of the night, see him popping those Aleves 24/7.

When he gets to my seat, he takes a little breather, says, "Too much coffee."

"You need some help, Gramp?"

He waves off the offer. "I'm not that old yet," he tells me. "Just need to take my time—it's greasy going." Then he winks at Purplehead. "My grandson's a good boy. Don't corrupt him."

You'd think she'd be offended, but she just about blasts my ear off with that big laugh of hers. "Glad to see someone in your family has a sense of humor," she tells Gramp, and the two of them think that's even funnier.

Gramp continues on, but not before he whispers to me, "She speaks the language."

For Gramp, that's a big compliment, and he don't give it out often. Usually saves it for his friends from Portland High, or guys he worked with at S. D. Warren, people he trusts; you know, someone who ain't fake, who won't lie, will give it to you straight. Kinda blows me away he'd say it about her.

I turn in my seat, watch him make his way to the back. He stops by the jocks; probably asking about the game. Can't hear him, but I bet he's giving them the rundown of who's gonna win and why. Although football's his fave, Gramp follows all the sports, even golf. Since he retired from the mill, no matter what the weather or how far away the school is, Gramp never misses any of my games. My basketball team calls him *Our Fan*, for he's always there, most of the time even before we are. We'll get off the bus and walk into the gym, and there'll be Gramp sitting in the empty bleachers, scoutin' out the other team warming up. During a game, yuh can always hear him—*Box out! Press 'em! Nice shot!* And if we're playing lousy, *Get your head in the game, boys!* Or at our coach, *How many times you gonna let him throw the ball away before you take him out!*

Gramp says things were different when he was a kid, says back then coaches didn't coddle anyone, that's the word he likes to use, *coddle*. He says if a kid screws up, you gotta ream him out, let him sit on the bench and think about what he did wrong, so when he goes back in, he don't make the same mistake. He says *if you don't hold a kid accountable they'll never learn to get better*. He'll yap your ear off on stuff like that, and how parents these days give winning a bad name. He calls them *fun-for-alls*. Ma won't even sit next to him if she comes to one of my games, says she *can't stand listening to his running commentary*. But I know it's more than that. See, Gramp thinks if my parents hadn't let Derek quit playing sports, he wouldn't have had time to get in trouble, wouldn't be where he is now.

'Sides, Gramp don't believe in quitting at nothing. Don't matter if it's too dark to see when I'm mowing his lawn or if my team's down by twenty with a minute left on the clock, he'll be yelling, *Stick with it!* He still don't get it that Derek couldn't. Says all my brother needed was *a good kick in the pants to set him straight*.

I turn my back on Gramp and the B-ball boys he's still yukking it up with, and feel like pounding something. Wish my parents had just said screw work and come with me. I love Gramp, don't get me wrong, but he can really grind my gears sometimes. Like how he'll say stuff about my parents, how they should've put their foot down, should've done this, should've done that. There's a whole freakin' list, and, let me tell yuh, I'm gettin' some tired of listening to it. Thinks he's the big expert, but he never had to live with my brother, doesn't have a clue what Derek's really like when one of those bad moods hits us like a freight train. Has never seen him like we have, never met that stranger I have nightmares of, the one who wrecks furniture and beats the crap outta me with his fists and words, the one who can't sleep, who paces like those lions in their cages down in York: back and forth, back and forth, freakin' all night long.

Easy for Gramp to believe Derek's still his golden boy; he's never seen him when he gets that look in his eyes that tells me I'd better run for cover if I don't wanna get stitches again, that stare that lets me know Derek's left the building and I'd better beat it to the bathroom and lock the door 'cause something's gonna get broken, someone's gonna get hurt. Don't matter how much they coulda, woulda, shoulda put their foot down, nothing's gonna change things when he gets like that. Yell, beg, threaten, cry, call the cops: don't matter, it just don't.

"What's your problem?" asks Purplehead, and it takes me a second to realize she's staring down at my fist, that somehow she knows I'm ready to punch something or somebody.

"Hope you're not mad about what I said to your grandfather," she tells me. "If you are, you need to lighten up. I was just messing with him."

Way she says it makes me laugh, makes me tell her the truth. "I'm not mad 'bout that. I thought it was funny. So did he."

She smiles, and I notice her front teeth don't line up with the crease in her top lip or with the tip of her nose, that though the teeth are straight, they're slightly off center. It bugs me, like a crooked picture on a wall, makes me wanna fix it.

"That's good," she says. "I'd have to find another seat if you couldn't take a joke."

"You could always sit next to that guy back there," I tell her, nodding in the direction of BO. "Bet that kid with the green face would pay yuh to switch."

She follows my stare then turns around and nails me in the arm. "*So* not nice."

"Chill," I tell her. "Just joking." Guess there's no messin' with Marvel Girl. Those bony knuckles of hers hurt worse than Derek's. I wanna rub my arm wicked bad, but she'll think I'm a wuss.

"Besides, you never know," she says, "he might have a good story."

"Huh?"

She don't answer, just sits there zombie gazing. Not sure if she's thinking or didn't hear me. "Hello? Anyone home?"

With her eyes still glued to the grimy gray seat in front of us, she says, "Like, maybe he used to be rich. You know, had it all—gorgeous wife, two kids, one of those summer mansions in Camden my Memere cleans from June to September. Then, one day, his wife and kids were killed in a car accident, and he loved them so much it just tore him apart, so he stopped going to work, stopped paying his bills, and that's the reason he got fired from his million-dollar job and why the bank took his cars and his houses and why he's trying to drink himself to death. And now he's riding on a Greyhound bus instead of driving a black Porsche."

She turns and looks at me. "Isn't that wicked sad?" Then she flashes her off-centered smile, tells me, "That's what I'm talking about."

Blows me away how she did that, how she made me believe it could almost be true. "Sweet," I tell her.

"Yeah," she agrees. "But most likely, he's an alcoholic like my uncle who's never worked a day in his life, so there's no way I'm sitting next to that dirtbag."

I'm startin' to like this girl.

"So what about you?" she wants to know. "What's your story?"

My story? She wouldn't want me to lay it on her. See, when you got a brother with a mental illness, people don't wanna hear about it. It slays me, 'cause if Derek had cancer or some disease like that kid with leukemia at the church we used to go to, people would feel sorry for him. They'd send him cards and visit him in the hospital. They'd have church suppers and put donation cans in the 7-Eleven and raise enough money for a family trip to freakin' Disney World.

It's true.

If Derek had cancer, they wouldn't put him on a waitin' list for five months to see some shrink who, Ma finds out in the newspaper four months later, got sued and lost his license. Wouldn't make him wait a million hours in the ER after he goes postal or tell my parents he can't be admitted 'cause they don't got enough beds or make my dad leave for yelling, *If he had a broken leg, you'd find him a goddamn bed fast enough!*

But that's the way it is; that's the way it works. Unless yuh brother slices himself with a box cutter, yuh better bring your PSP—gonna be sitting in the waiting room forever.

"So?" she asks. "Are you going to tell me your story, or what?"

"I don't have one."

But she won't take no for an answer 'cause someday she's gonna make movies. "C'mon," she says, like that little kid Leo begging for dibs. "Everybody has something to hide."

"Say what?"

"That's what Ms. Cofran, my English teacher, is always telling us. She says the best stories are the ones people try to hide, you know, like *Ethan Frome*? She's had some stuff published, too, so she knows what she's talking about. She's awesome; I love her. She's the only good teacher we have at our school, and she's leaving."

"Why?" I ask, not that I give a rip; I just want Purplehead to leave me alone, don't want her to know what I got hiding in New Jersey.

"She's going to teach next year at some private academy down in Connecticut. Her big excuse is: It pays a lot more and they give her a place to live. But everyone in town knows the real story. See, she was supposed to get married this summer, had everything all planned—date, church, blah, blah, blah, and then . . ."

Purplehead's all wound up, and I let her rattle, pretend I'm listening like Dad does when Ma gets rantin' about *That Thievin' Insurance Company*. Ma hates them so bad she can go on for hours. Heard it so much, know it by heart: *It's a mortal sin what they've done to our family! We've been paying them out of your check every week for eighteen years, but as soon as one of our kids needs help, it's he has a mental illness, read the fine print, a hundred grand for a lifetime, that's all we pay, that's all he gets! Took us about half of that just to get the right diagnosis. Didn't even take three years to reach their magic number—not when an eight-day stay at Winstonbrook costs* sixteen thousand a pop, not when you're in and out of the ER like it's your second home. Then they bury us in paperwork, hoping we'll go away. Make us fill out ten thousand forms not even a doctor or a lawyer can understand, knowing most people will just give up. It's not right. It just isn't right.

Then to read in the paper the CEO of that insurance company in Portland got a six-hundred-thousand-dollar bonus? That's the final slap in the face, let me tell you. Here, we've lost everything—our son, our house, our savings—we go mentally and financially bankrupt, and that son of a gun gets a six-hundred-thousand-dollar bonus? Am I wrong here? I mean, you don't have to be a genius to connect the thievin' dots!

That's just the tip-off. Trust me. When Ma starts in, I get outta there fast as I can. So does Gramp; he beats feet for the front porch with a couple of cigars, for he knows he's gonna be there a long time. *Your mother's on her bandwagon* is how he likes to put it.

"Isn't that awful?" asks Purplehead.

I nod, but have no idea what she's talking about or how long she's been going. Ever notice that? How girls can talk forever about nothing? Or like Ma, about the same thing over and over. I mean, I hate that insurance company, too. Hate how it screwed my brother outta the help he needed. Hate how it turned our kitchen into a war zone night after night.

How filling out all those stupid forms was the number one thing in my parents' lives and their number one excuse for everything, like missing my science fair—even the sports night when I got the trophy for outstanding player.

But even more than everything *That Thievin' Insurance Company* did to my brother and my family and me, the thing I hate most is hearing about it over and over and over. Can't even have a meal or watch a TV show or go to the grocery store without it coming up. Ma will work *That Thievin' Insurance Company* into the conversation somehow, and that's why our old neighbors and relatives and even her best friend, Amy, don't want to be around her no more, 'cause, like me, they're freakin' tired of that bandwagon.

Purplehead nudges me with her elbow to make a point or make sure I'm paying attention. "I think Ms. Cofran's lucky he dumped her for that nurse from Lewiston," she tells me. "I mean, once a cheater, always a cheater, that's what Oprah says. It's better to find that out before you say 'I do' and have kids and have to get divorced like my—"

She suddenly stops talking and it's her silence and how she looks away from me that really get my attention. What I saw in her eyes before she turned toward the window would be hard to draw, but I think I could do it.

"I hear yuh," I tell her, for though the reason ain't the

same, I know that look. I've seen it in the mirror: even nailed it once in a self-portrait while Derek was on a rampage and I was stuck in the bathroom with nothing to do and nothing to use but a tube of Ma's lipstick and the tile on the shower wall.

"I'm never getting married," mumbles Purplehead, still staring at her reflection in the black window. "I'd never do that to a kid."

"Ditto," I tell her, for from what I've read online, it runs in families, could get passed along like a big nose. Made me wonder if that's why my aunt, who no one ever mentions, committed suicide in college. Makes me afraid they'll find Derek with a belt around his neck hanging from a water pipe like her. Makes me scared to fall asleep at night 'cause, being his brother, and the same age he was when he really started to change, I might wake up some morning and be just like him.

I feel a hand grip my shoulder, and it pulls me outta that nightmare in my head and almost outta my seat.

"Didn't mean to scare you," says Gramp.

"I wasn't scared," I lie. "Just forgot you were back there."

"Been talking with those boys," he tells me. "Maybe next time we can spend the night in Boston and catch a game. I haven't done that since Larry Bird."

"That'd be awesome," I tell him, though next time I'm gonna beg my parents to take me.

"Better get back to my seat," says Gramp. "Newburyport should be coming right up."

CHAPTER 6

The whole time Derek's been gone, I only got one letter. It came two days before Halloween, and Ma was already asking to read it before I even got the envelope open. Couldn't get past the first sentence 'cause of her: *What'd he say? What'd he say? What'd he say?*

That'd tick you off, wouldn't it?

Told her, "It's my freakin' letter!"

Know that shocked her; shocked me, too. Unlike Derek, I never swear around Ma. That's the way it is in our house, Derek can drop the F-bomb all he wants 'cause of his *disorder*; me, I say the word *fart* and get whacked upside the head. But that time, Ma just gave me a look that felt worse than the whack I'd expected. You know that mother look, the one that makes yuh feel guilty and sorry and dirtier than pond scum all at the same time—the one that's followed up with *God, what have I done to deserve this?*

But for once in my life, I didn't give in, didn't go clean my room for her or wash the dishes or mow the lawn. Didn't let her read my letter. Carried it around in my back pocket like a wallet, read it so many times it fell apart. Had to put the Scotch tape to it and hide it in the suitcase I use for a drawer at Gramp's.

From his letter, the place Derek's at sounds worse than the army. Has to make his bed a certain way and do the same stuff every day at the same exact time. Says it's so bad he even takes a dump on schedule.

Thing is, can't even picture Derek makin' a bed. He never helped out around the house like I do, always got out of it somehow. Whenever Ma got on one of her cleaning campaigns, he'd head for the hills. Come up with something he had to do or someplace he had to go, and I'd get sucked into doing his share. *I'll pay yuh later, Zach.* Right—like that ever happened.

So I'm thinking maybe it's good that they make him do stuff like that. If he was home, he probably wouldn't even get out of bed, let alone make it. Think I'm kidding? Sometimes he'd live in his cave for days. Ma never liked me calling his room that, but that's what it was. Always dark, shades down, lights off. Stole a KEEP OUT sign from a construction site on Commercial Street, nailed it on his door so none of us would go in. Not that you'd want to—smelled worse than the Altmans' dog when it had that skin disease. Ma told me I'd need a tetanus shot if I walked around in there barefoot. Couldn't even see the carpet 'cause of all the clothes and paper plates and Mountain Dew cans—always felt like there was a fork buried in one of those piles just waitin' to stick me. When Derek was *feeling low,* as Ma likes to put it, he'd hole up in his cave and only come out to get food or use the bathroom or yell at us to shut the F up. Sometimes he'd sleep so long I'd sneak in there to make sure he was still breathing. The times Derek was in silent mode and would sleep forever were almost as scary as when he was having a meltdown and breaking the furniture. That lump under the covers whining—*my life sucks; I wish I was dead; you'd be better off without me—* wasn't my brother. My brother was the Derek who could make anybody laugh, who everybody loved; the *hottie* who could really play drums, the Derek who was so sure of himself, he wasn't afraid of nothin' or nobody.

"Wonder how much snow we're supposed to get?" says Purplehead, sounding worried.

I lean over to take a look but can barely see out the window. Hadn't even been spitting when we'd left, and now we're in the middle of a blizzard. "Must be drivin' into the storm," I tell her. "Reminds me of last week when me and my dad were comin' back from Augusta. We leave there, right? The roads are all bare, and not a snowflake in the sky. Hit Brunswick, there's three inches on the ground. By Portland, it's a total whiteout. Traffic was backed up so bad, took us over an hour to drive one mile. Found out later it was 'cause a tractor trailer jackknifed on Tukey's Bridge near B&M Beans."

"That makes me feel a whole lot better," she says. "Not!"

"No worries," I tell her. "Got a lot more protection on a bus than in a car."

"Didn't help those people in Mexico," she barks at me. "Two buses crashed into each other, and twenty-five people were killed. Just happened, like, two days ago."

Any other good news?

"I mean, we don't even have seat belts—what's up with that?" she wants to know. "The only reason my mother's alive is because she was wearing her seat belt."

"Was she in a car accident?"

Purplehead nods. "A really bad one. She stopped for a light that was turning red, but the idiot cement truck driver behind her thought she was going to run it. He hit her so hard it pushed her car right through the intersection. They had to use the Jaws of Life to get her out. It was awful. She broke her leg and had to wear a neck brace, but the scariest thing was the concussion."

Purplehead likes to use her hands when she talks and right now taps her forehead with two fingers. "It gave her short-term memory loss. I'd tell her something, and ten minutes later, she'd forget it, wouldn't even remember talking to me. It was like living with Mrs. Chase, who has Alzheimer's. I was petrified she'd turn the stove on and forget about it and burn the house down. Hands down—worst summer of my life. First my father splits on us kids and then my mother can't even remember who we are."

She says that last part like she's making a joke, but it don't feel like one.

"Is she all right now?" I ask.

"When it's raining or cold out, her neck still hurts her, but the concussion thing only lasted about three weeks—thank God for that." She rolls her eyes, then slowly shakes her head, like she's back there remembering it all. "I don't know how Mr. Chase does it. I'd be a nutbag if I had to take care of his wife."

Try living with my brother when he's having an *episode*, I feel like telling her, but I hafta keep that stuff to myself. Don't even talk about that with Frankie, and we've been best buds since we could walk.

"It'd make a good Lifetime movie, though," says Purplehead. "They could call it *Chasing Mrs. Chase,* because, swear to God, at least once a month, the whole town's out hunting for her. She's pretty crafty; Mr. Chase has to watch her like a hawk."

The bus slows down as it takes the exit, and just as we come out of the curve, the back end fishtails and bangs the guardrail. Purplehead latches on to my arm; Joey squeals "wheee!" and his baby sister wakes up howling.

"Sorry for the little curtsy, folks," says the driver after pulling the bus out of its skid. "Must've hit a patch of ice under that new snow."

"Hey, dude, thanks a lot!" Poor Schmuck tells BO, as he wipes the wine off his jacket. "Like my mother's gonna believe *that* happened. No way I'll pass her sniff test now."

"My Cheez-Its!"

"I'll get 'em for you, lady," shouts Leo, who takes a handful before sliding the box back down the aisle bowling ball–style.

The baby's screaming feels like a blade stabbing into my ears, but I don't wanna cover them 'cause Purplehead still has a death grip on my arm and it's making me feel like a hero.

"Be just a few minutes for those getting off at Newburyport," the driver says, so calmly you'd never know we almost went off the road two seconds ago. "Those passengers traveling on to Boston please remain on the bus."

"Sorry I grabbed you," says Purplehead, letting go of me.

"No problem, Marvel Girl. Wolverine's here to protect you."

She laughs, asks, "Which one's Wolverine?"

The one Jean Grey—aka Marvel Girl—is in love with. "Show you when we stop," I tell her, for I can't take the pain no more, hafta cover my ears.

One of the green-face boys in the back can't take it, either, asks loud enough for even me to hear under my handmuffs, "Can't she give that kid a bottle?"

It's a good question, as far as I'm concerned, but Purplehead lives on another planet. Next thing I know, she's hangin' over my lap with her head in the aisle. "The baby has an earache," she tells him. "Try to be nice, even if you're not."

The B-ball boys think that's hilarious. One of them says, "You're right, we can't take him anywhere. Why don't you come back here and teach him some manners?"

"Get a life," she shoots back. "Get nine of them."

"I think she likes you, Walt. Maybe you can ask her to the winter ball."

"Like you already got a date."

Purplehead sits back in her seat, eyes ready to kill, nostrils wiggling like the Cadbury Bunny. "Jock-holes."

Don't know what her problem is; she's the one who started that pissin' match. "Watch it," I tell her. "I live to play basketball."

"Figures," she says, then whips on her headphones, snaps open her *Rolling Stone*, and pretends to read.

Guess she's done talking to me.

The bus station's right off the highway in the middle of nowhere. Looks so deserted I'm thinking it's closed, but I'm praying to Jesus Leo's *Aunty* owns one of the two cars in the parking lot. As the bus rolls to a stop, I glance down the aisle, but it don't look like he's gettin' his coat on.

The young couple who were all over each other at the bus station must've been hoping, too. Above the baby's screeching, I hear the guy tell his girlfriend, "Nope. They're not getting off."

Over the mic, the driver says, "On account of the weather, we're running a little behind, folks, but this should be a quick stop. Once again, those traveling on to Boston and South Station please remain in your seats. For those departing, check to make sure you have all your belongings."

This time when the door opens, the cold air leaking in feels wicked good. Helps get rid of some of the gross old-people smells and the dump-whiffs I keep gettin' from that load in Joey's Pampers.

I see Gramp stand up and figure he's gotta go again, but he's just letting the man in the seat beside him out. The man shakes Gramp's hand like they've been friends for life instead of an hour, and, as he makes his way to the front of the bus, I grab my stuff and escape while I got the chance.

"I'm back, Gramp."

He looks up as if he's surprised to see me. "When you can sit with a pretty girl? What's the matter with you, Zach?"

With all the noise, I don't think anyone heard him, but just the possibility makes me wanna melt right into the floor. Thing is, Gramp ain't moving; he actually expects an answer. I put my hand against his good ear and whisper the only excuse I got for being a loser. "She hates jocks."

He nods, says, "Your grandmother did, too."

When he stands up to let me have the window, I slide in as fast as I can, then sneak a look back through the seats. No way she heard him—saved by Bawling Baby!

Still, it was a close call. *When you can sit with a pretty girl?* Cripe, he's worse than Ma, and she's the master—still tries to kiss me good-bye in front of my friends. Then adults wonder why yuh don't wanna be seen with them in public.

Gramp clears his throat, and that phlegm-rattle of his

ticks me off even more. Have another cigar, I wanna tell him. For real, I'm never gonna smoke, don't care how cool it makes you look. Way Derek's going, he's gonna die of lung cancer before he's thirty—started smoking when he was about ten. No joke, caught him and Howie out in the tree fort puffing on one of Dad's Marlboro Lights. Now he don't even care that my parents know, sometimes lights up right in front of them just to show who's boss. Likes to tell Dad, *It's your secondhand smoke that got me addicted.* Always gotta be someone else's fault with Derek. *Now look what you made me do* is what he told me after he threw that steak knife when I was eating potato chips too loud. Course he came up with a big elaborate story when we saw I was gonna need some stitches. That time we told Ma I was looking for something to eat in the fridge while he was getting ice cream outta the freezer and, when I stood up, I cracked my forehead on the freezer's handle where the metal thing's broken. Parents will believe anything.

"Interesting fella, that man I was just sitting with," Gramp says when he's done with his coughing attack. "Retired nurse, imagine that. He had a career in the navy working with surgeons and explained my plumbing condition better than my own doctor did. Gave me a couple of names of people I should go see in Portland."

I can hardly hear Gramp over Bawling Baby. Should tell Mrs. West to make a tape of that howling for her sex ed. class. It's curing me of ever wanting to do it without protection. Be better than those stupid egg babies she tried to make us haul around for a week. Talk about a joke. Only one whose egg survived was Velma Pelletier's, and even hers had a crack in it. My egg baby didn't even live long enough to name it. About thirty seconds after Mrs. West gave it to me, it rolled right off my desk while I was picking up a pencil.

I plug my fingers in my ears and start humming to drown out Bawling Baby. What I wanna know is where the hell is Dumbledore? I mean, only one guy got off, and no one else seems to be getting on. Probably taking a break from the noise—lucky him!

Bet he's using a real bathroom while he's got the chance.

And having a soda and a Snickers outta one of those vending machines, and—

Gramp nudges me, and I remove the finger from my right ear to listen.

"I feel so bad for that poor baby," he tells me, "but it's giving me a headache right between the eyes."

"I know. Wish they were gettin' off here."

"That fella I was talking with said she could rupture an eardrum."

Whose? "Mine?"

Gramp chuckles. "No, son, not yours; hers."

"Sure feels like it could."

"I'll tell you, an earache's the worst pain there is," says Gramp. "I had so many infections as a kid that I can't hear worth a damn out of this ear."

It's the first time I've heard that story. Usually Gramp says he lost his hearing when he got married.

"I had to put lamb's wool in my ears every time I went swimming."

I don't have a clue what Gramp means by that. I've found that when he gets going on something you don't understand, best thing to do is nod your head and pretend you do, or he'll spend the next hour trying to explain it.

With the driver gone, Leo and Joey figure it's the perfect time to make a food run. They race down the aisle and start their begging at the back of the bus, Leo using the same line on everyone. "'Scuse me, you got any snacks maybe you can share with me and my brother?"

I turn around and kneel on my seat to watch them.

One of the B-ball boys gives Leo a buck to "get lost."

BO growls at them like a dog that ain't gonna share his food dish, and Suitcase pretends he don't know English again.

They score some pretzels off the Suck-Face Couple, but mostly people just ignore them, pretend those two rug rats begging for food ain't talking to them. If Ma was here, she'd definitely give 'em something to eat. Knowing her, she'd take right over; probably change Joey's pants without even asking permission.

When they finally get to Purplehead, Leo wants to know, "Where'd Cookie Boy go?"

I duck outta sight and try to use Gramp as a shield to make myself invisible. They've already got my sandwich and Doritos; like Dad tells those cashiers when they ask for donations at the register, *I already gave at the office.*

Right before they get to me and Gramp, the driver returns, brushing off snow as he climbs aboard.

"Quick, Joey!" Leo warns. "He's back!"

They race by us, and I lean over just in time to see Joey hit the deck facefirst, an apple launching outta his hand like a grenade. Now he's bawling louder than his sister.

"Leo!" yells their mother, who's trapped in her seat by the baby every person on this bus wants to strangle. "Help him up!"

Leo tries by wrapping his arms around Joey's waist, but the kid's head's gotta weigh thirty pounds, and there ain't no way Leo can lift him.

"Hurry," says his mother, then threatens, "or you two will be walking to Aunty's in this snowstorm."

I can tell Leo's scared by the look on his face, but he's had enough. "I'm just a kid!" he yells at her. "Whaddaya want?"

Thinking that question was meant for him, Joey wails, "My a-a-ap-ple!"

"Forget about it," Leo snaps and, latching on to one of Joey's arms, starts tugging his brother's body down the aisle. The poor kid's sweatshirt's riding up so his bare belly scrapes along the floor.

I need to help them, but before I can get past Gramp, Purplehead's flying by, and once again, it's Marvel Girl to the rescue.

Jazzed I no longer hafta help, I sit back down and listen to the sound of her voice, a mix of mother and teacher—a baby-sitter used to being in charge. Bet her little sisters love her, bet she plays games with them and junk like that. Can just tell by how she says, "Man down! Quick, Leo, we need to get Joey back to the spaceship before it takes off!"

Who'd think of that? Not me. Maybe if I was six or some-thing. But it works. The two ankle biters are back in their seats before the driver even puts it in reverse.

I catch a glimpse of her as she goes back down the aisle, and now I'm wishin' I hadn't moved. Gramp's right; something must be wrong with me.

CHAPTER 7

Back on the highway, the driving's ten times worse. Yellow lights flash the speed limit at forty-five, but those eighteen-wheelers poundin' us with slush don't give a rip. Every time one whizzes by, the whole bus starts shaking and swaying. Still, guess we should thank those truckers for rocking Bawling Baby back to sleep.

I shut off my light so I can see outside better and start counting cars that have run off the road; seven already. Some have cops already there, some don't, some are smashed up, some just buried in the shoulder. A van facing the opposite direction—half on the median, half in the passing lane—almost gets clipped by an SUV.

"Jesus!" someone yells. "Didja see that?"

"Lucky!" someone else answers, and now everyone's talkin' in whispers and flicking off their lights so they can see the show.

The driver tells us not to use the restroom till road conditions are better, and no one needs an explanation. Seriously, who'd wanna be in that box with their pants down around their boots like Leo if this thing crashes?

Can hear it now: "He died pinching a loaf on a Greyhound." Or, knowing my friends: "Bet Zach was in there whackin' off."

And just like that, there's a picture in my head—priest reading from a Bible, people crying around my grave, Frankie Altman whispering behind his hand to Tony Nappi, "Least he died doing somethin' he liked."

Doubt Miss Lott would let me draw that one for the *Roundtable*. She's already shot down three of mine. *Inappropriate* is her favorite word. Says my drawings are amazing but my humor's *inappropriate* for a school newspaper. Screw her.

"Should've known we were in for a storm," says Gramp. "My knee's been aching all day."

Up ahead I see red and blue lights, the combo of flashing color through fallin' snow like being in Funtown's Astrosphere. "Number eight," I tell Gramp.

"Looks like a bad one," he answers.

There's only one lane open, and the bus is crawling behind a line of tractor trailers. We're going so slow we can see sparks in the flares and the car laying on its side with two wheels in the air and the silhouette of rescue workers haulin' a stretcher toward a vehicle that kinda looks like Gramp's LeSabre.

"Momma!" cries Joey. "I scared!"

"It's okay, baby. You and Leo come sit with me and Sister—but don't wake her up."

A state trooper, his Smokey Bear hat bent against the blowing snow, is breaking out the back window with a crowbar. It's in slo-mo and don't seem real, like what I'm watching's right out of a movie. As if he's feeling the same way as me, BO drops the F-bomb and yells, "Where am I?"

"Florida," says Poor Schmuck. "Go back to sleep and stop breathing on me, dude."

I start wondering if I'll ever see New Jersey, start thinking it's a good thing my parents didn't come. Who'd take care of Derek if something ever happened to them?

"Great. We'll be lucky if we make it by halftime," says one of the B-ball boys, and one of his buddies tells him, "Shut up, Chappy. Might be someone killed in that accident."

"One of those dang tractor trailers probably ran it off the road" is Cheez-It's theory.

I lean over Gramp to catch a glimpse of Purplehead, but like everyone else, she's got her light off, and I can't make her out.

"Gramp, maybe I should go sit with that girl. She's probably scared; her mother was in a wicked bad car accident a couple of years ago."

The King of Fender Benders says, "That's terrible," and I know he means it. "Go ahead," he tells me. "But be quick about it, Zach, the driver doesn't want folks walking around."

Purplehead doesn't even notice when I slip into the seat beside her. By the way her head's tilted forward, for a second I think she's sleeping, but then I hear her whispering. From all those years of Ma dragging us to church, I know the Our Father when I hear it. Praying's private. I shouldn't be listening. Smooth move, Quagmire—what now? Tap her on the elbow so she knows I'm here? Cough? And what if she's like Ma and don't wanna be interrupted? Seriously, if we bugged Ma during Mass, she'd give us a look that'd nail you to the cross or a pinch that'd make your eyes water. Ma's a die-hard fan when it comes to God 'cause she went to Catholic schools and one of her uncles is a priest. Derek likes to tease her about it, calls her the *Blessless Mother*. He says church ain't nothing but a bunch of old people sitting around telling fairy tales, says the only reason he used to go was for the free doughnuts after Mass. He quit soon as he made his confirmation, and me and Ma quit last year after the new priest came 'cause all he ever talks about is *money, money, money*. So now Ma tells everyone she's gonna be a heathen for a while, says when attendance at church gets down low enough, they'll get rid of him and she'll go back.

I reach up and turn the light on.

It works—she stops praying, says, "I hope those people are okay."

"Me, too," I tell her, for even though the accident's behind us now, I can still picture that car laying on its side like a dead bug, its Maine license plate caught in the glare of lights—*Vacationland*.

"That car looked almost as bad as my mother's."

Maybe Miss Lott's right—*inappropriate humor*—but my fingers are really itching for a pencil. *Vacationland*. Why is that so funny to me?

"I still have nightmares about it. What was Uncle Mickey thinking?" asks Purplehead, like I'm supposed to know what she's talking about.

"I can't believe he took me down there. If my mother knew, she'd have a fit and then some. But I had to get my math book. That's why I went with Uncle Mickey when he cleaned out the car—to get my stupid math book."

"Oh" is the only bright thing I can think to say.

"They towed it to a place in Camden. When I first saw it, I thought, How did Mom live? No exaggeration. The back end was crunched so bad it looked like a Pepsi can someone stomped on. Really, I'm not kidding. The only thing I could see through the shattered window was Katherine's head."

I remember the faces, hair, new school clothes of those girls in the picture, and get a gross feeling in my stomach. "Who's Katherine?" I ask, hoping it's not one of her sisters, whose names I forgot as soon as she told me.

"Lindsey's doll," she answers. "She left it in the car. I never told her, though. My sister was in love with that ugly thing. She'd been dragging it around since she was two, had gnawed off all the fingers. With those creepy marble eyes and ratty hair, looked like something out of a Chucky movie. Whenever Lindsey slept in my bed, it'd scare the hell out of me to wake up and see that thing resting on my pillow, but seeing Katherine's head smashed like a pancake between the seat and the door was a million times worse. It made me know for real that if my mother'd had my little sisters with her, they'd be dead. . . . And there's my uncle with his camera, taking goddamn pictures like a flatlander tourist. Can you believe that?"

"It's for the insurance company," I tell her. "Trust me, I

know. My gramp's in a car accident 'bout every other week. He keeps a disposable camera in his glove box just for that."

"But he didn't have to do it in front of me. That mangled wreck was our car. You know?"

It makes me wonder if Dad should have taken a picture of Derek—if they'll pay for a car that's wrecked, why not a person? Maybe if the insurance company had seen the blood, and Derek laying there, they wouldn't have cut him off when he reached their magic number.

"I lost my breakfast right there in the parking lot. I mean, my mother's blood was still on the steering wheel. Think she wanted people seeing a picture of that!?"

Even in the dim light, I can see the daggers in Purplehead's eyes, and I know she's right—Derek wouldn't want anyone seeing his blood on the floor, and neither would I.

"No one would," I tell her.

"She must have the flu," says Purplehead, and the voice she's imitating, I figure, must be her uncle's.

"That's what he told the guy that worked there. Moron or what? I didn't get sick because of that; it was him shooting with his camera from every angle like our car was a national monument. It was no flu; it was watching him get down on his knees for a better picture of how Mom lost the baby."

"Baby?"

"She was pregnant."

Sorry ain't enough. Sorry ain't nothin'. "That sucks," I tell her.

"If I'd had a gun, I would have killed him."

I hear her; I got a hit list of my own.

Like that witch at the insurance place. She was so nasty to Ma, I wanted to jump over the counter and punch her face in. *It doesn't work that way, Mrs. Andersen. We don't deal with that sort of thing here,* blah, blah, blah, like Ma was some dumb lowlife. Ms. Marshall with her weasel face and lipstick on her teeth didn't give a rip that the number on the back of Ma's insurance card was always busy or put her on hold for eternity, she wasn't gonna be the real person Ma needed to talk to.

"I would've killed him, too," I tell Purplehead.

She gives a weak laugh, says, "You'd have to get in line behind a few other people." Then she pulls out a tissue—*Have Kleenex, will travel.*

Feel wicked bad for her, but can't help wondering what it's like, blowing your nose when yuh got a diamond in there. Can tell by the way she shoves that wadded ball into her pocket when she's all done, ain't the time to ask.

"Didn't mean to go Debbie Downer on you," she tells me, her voice almost back to normal. "Just seeing that accident, all those cars off the road. Look at my hand—it's shaking worse than the Lion's in *The Wizard of Oz*."

She's wearing a ring shaped like a snake, and her fingernails are painted black, but I like it that she can be funny when she's so scared. Makes me wanna protect her, makes me brave enough to touch her—her skin's soft, her fingers ice-cold.

"Don't worry," I tell her. "We'll be all right."

She stares down at my hand on hers, and now I'm the one who's afraid—can she tell I chew my fingernails till they bleed? Should I tell her that black stuff's from the sketch I did and not dirt?

But she doesn't seem to notice, doesn't try to pull her hand away, just admits, "I've never told anyone about that. Not even my sisters."

I know where she's coming from, 'cause I'm an expert at keeping secrets. I could work for the FBI. "You couldn't," I tell her. "Sometimes you can't." You just have to live with it, try to keep your lies straight—*he's working construction for my uncle in New Jersey.*

I'm still holding her hand when the bus crashes.

CHAPTER 8

One second we're riding along 95, then—*BAM!*—we're plowing through a snowbank.

Driving along, and—*WHAM!*—we're buried in some field in the pitch-dark.

For a moment, it's so quiet you can hear the snow.

CHAPTER 9

Then all hell breaks loose.

People moaning.

Crying.

Yelling.

"I can't see!"

"Momma!"

"My neck!"

The dark's alive with voices, but there's only one I wanna
hear—"Gramp!"

The girl's glued to me, trapping me, her fingernails cuttin'
into my skin. I pull her claws off of my neck and shove her
away—I need to move, need to know if he's all right. I crawl

my way through the dark, patting the floor as I inch ahead, listening for his answer.

"Is anybody hurt?"

"I think I'm bleeding."

"No bars here!"

"Zach?"

The driver shines a flashlight down the aisle, and it blinds me. "Everyone stay in your seats!"

Screw him. I stand up, walk the last couple of steps.

"Please, folks, no one panic..."

"You okay, Gramp?" I ask, trying to read his face in the dark.

"Knocked my noggin, but everything seems to be working. You?"

It's only then that I taste the blood in my mouth. I find the tender spot with my tongue then lean over and spit. "Yuh; just bit my lip."

The driver sweeps the bus with his flashlight as he makes his way toward the back, asking over and over, "Anyone hurt? Anyone hurt?"

"I'm bleeding," says one of the B-ball boys. "My nose. I need Kleenex."

I turn in my seat just in time to see the light shine on the kid's face—he ain't lying, looks like a bottle of Heinz exploded on him.

"Hang on, son," the driver tells him. "I'll get some for you; just tilt your head back against the seat."

From somewhere inside my head, I remember: first aid kit—left-hand rack.

"Must've been snoozing," says Gramp. "Didn't know where I was or what hit me."

I can barely hear Gramp with Joey and his baby sister bawling in full throttle and Cheez-It moaning about her neck and Dumbledore gettin' bombarded with stupid questions— "Have you called the police yet?" "What's the next exit?" "Where are we?" "What happened?"

"Give me a minute, please!" he shouts, rushing by with a first aid kit in one hand, flashlight in the other. "I need to help this boy first."

"Too bad that nurse got off at the last stop," says Gramp, then, rubbing his hand against the window, tells me, "Can't see for beans."

Actually, I can see better now that my eyes are adjusting to the dark. Can't make out faces, but can sort of see people, like the person stumbling down the aisle past me.

"Wonder where they think they're going?" I ask Gramp.

"The bathroom?" is his guess, but that'd be in the wrong direction.

"I need to go so bad, I'm ready to whiz out the window," Gramp whispers. "You still have that soda bottle?"

I don't even have a chance to think how gross that'd be, 'cause someone starts pounding on the door.

"That was quick," I tell Gramp, thinking help's already arrived. But then I hear "Let me out! I'm going to be sick!" and realize it's not help banging on the door tryin' to get in—it's Purplehead tryin' to get out! She sounds like my cat before it hocks up a hairball, and her gagging noises on top of Gramp's dog-mess—smelling cigar breath is making me wanna hurl, too.

"Momma," Leo hollers, "if Clowngirl pukes on the bus, will he make her walk?"

Just like that, Joey quits his bawling to hear their mother answer, "Shut up and mind your own beeswax."

The only light on the bus gives us a laser show as the driver rockets up the aisle like Road Runner, and I'm thinking he can really move for an old guy.

"Ba-back up," he pants at Purplehead. "Can't . . . open doors . . . with you there."

She does what he tells her, and as soon as he pulls back the lever and the doors open, she bolts. The driver shines the light down the stairs, then follows her out into the storm.

In the back, BO starts dropping F-bombs 'cause he can't find his bag and demands, "Someone turn on the lights!"

"Even if it's stalled out, the lights should still work off the battery for a while," says Gramp. "I don't understand why they're not. Must have a short somewhere."

"I need my bag! Anyone see my—"

"Watch your language, please!" says Suitcase, and then reminds BO, "There's women and children present."

Cheez-It puts it to BO another way. "You kiss your mother with that mouth?"

People with cell phones are startin' to use 'em for flashlights, but no one's got service 'cause "We're in a dead zone," someone announces.

The driver climbs back on the bus, asks, "Anyone with that girl?"

"She's by herself," I tell him.

"Well, can someone come watch her while I check things out?"

The only one who volunteers is Gramp. "I will," he says, raising his hand.

I don't really wanna watch Purplehead throw up, but no way I'm gonna let Gramp stumble around in the dark and in the snow with his bad knee. "You stay here," I tell him, already moving toward the front. "She kinda knows me."

"Thanks," says the driver.

As I follow him down the stairs—the cold slapping me across the face before I'm even out the door—he warns, "She's really upset."

The bottom of the stairs barely clears the drift we've landed in. With that first step down, the snow's about up to my knees. The wind's wicked brutal, the sleety snow like needles prickin' into my skin. I try to follow in the footprints they've made 'cause I didn't listen to Ma and wear my boots. Only a geek wears boots, but it's a rule she don't get—I can already hear her: *How cool are you now, just wearing sneakers?*

I'm so *cool* I'm freakin' freezing! And an idiot for taking my hat off! That Gramp—gotta be a do-gooder. Now, besides gettin' bugs, I'm gonna freeze my ears off.

"Where'd she go?" The driver stops walking. "She was right here a minute ago." He flashes the light over the spot where Purplehead blew chunks, then shines it along the tracks leading away. "Mother of Jesus, this is all I need."

I look away from the bus, stare into the darkness—where's a streetlight when you need one? "Gimme the flashlight," I tell him. "I can find her faster than you."

"No, you get back on the bus, son. I can't have two passengers out in this mess; I've got enough trouble already." He shines the light over the back wheel that's buried. "Going to need a wrecker and a prayer to get this out."

I take a couple of steps beyond the bus, squint toward the road I can hear but can't see. My brain must be frozen, 'cause it don't make sense—what I can't see and what I can. Feels like I'm on the Tilt-A-Whirl ride; gotta hold my arms out just to keep my balance. I shut my eyes, then squint again, and *ding, ding, ding,* it all comes together like spottin' Waldo in a picture.

Snowbank!

That weird, foggy glow, appearing and disappearing: head-lights passing on the other side. The thing I thought was a flag waving in the wind: her.

"I see her!" I yell, pointing at Purplehead standing on top of that fence made of snow. "Up there!"

The snow beneath the new stuff's crusted but not strong enough to hold my weight, so I'm breakin' through with each step. By the time I crawl up the snowbank that feels like a mountain but ain't no taller than Ma, I'm sweatin' and my lungs are baked.

At the top, I can see the other side and the chances of one of those cars or tractor trailers going off the road, and it's a *worst way to die* that me and Frankie never thought of. But I'll never get to draw it—'cause it's me! I'm the King of the Mountain in the blizzard who's gonna be grille bait, mowed over by a sixteen-wheeler, crushed, mashed into the snow like a Frisbee you don't find till spring.

Something tugs on my sleeve, and there she is, wearing a hat of snow, clinging to my arm like a drunk, shouting over the wind and the sounds of wheels against snow, "What are you doing here?"

"I don't know," I answer. "Dreaming?"

"Exactly!" she yells back. "But we'll never wake up if we stay here!"

Next thing I know, she latches on to my hand and starts yanking me down the mountain. I get going so fast I can't stop. "Watch out!"

Mow her right over.

When I lift my face off her back, the driver's holding his light above us like the Statue of Liberty. "Got her," I tell him.

Maybe it's 'cause we're safer or it's the total weirdness of him and where we are, but we freakin' crack right up. Not sure how long me and Purplehead roll around in the snow laughing—him yellin' at us to stop our *shenanigans* and get back on the bus—but it's long enough that it hurts to breathe, long enough for her *we'll never wake up* joke to catch up to me, long enough for a huge guy to appear out of nowhere with a magnum searchlight and the news "Troopers and ambulance are on the way!"

I'm too dead from our laughing attack to move. I just lay there staring up at the Incredible Hulk while he tells the driver in a shaky voice, "I saw you go off the road; pulled my rig over as soon as I could." He shines his monster spotlight on me and Purplehead, then at the bus. "Everyone okay?"

"Got a kid with maybe a busted nose," says the bus driver. "Everyone's alive. That's all that counts."

"Amen to that. Wasn't sure what I'd find. It's a demolition derby out there. Lucky you slid off where you did."

While they're talking, me and Purplehead have the same idea—get out while the going's good. But just as we start sneaking off, the driver says, "Wait. Take this with you."

He slaps his flashlight into my hand, and that metal hitting against my frozen fingers kills. "That felt good!" I tell him. "Don't got no gloves on."

But he don't care about that. "Just get back on the bus," he says, like it's my fault I've risked my life and frozen my butt off to do him a favor.

"Kids," he tells Hulk, like that explains why I was out there rolling around in the snow.

"You're the one that drove us off the road," I remind him, tightening my grip, wanting to do what Derek already would've—hit him with the flashlight.

Ignoring me, he says to Purplehead, "Tell the passengers help's on the way."

"Let's go," she barks, grabbing the light from me. "I'm freezing."

The driver's already over us and talking with his new best bud about flares.

"That guy's lucky it's too cold to hit him," I tell Purplehead, but as I stomp along behind her, suddenly it's her I'm mad at. She's why my ears are ready to fall off and my feet are blocks of ice, why I'm even out in this crap!

"Where were you going?" I yell at her.

Passing the spot where she'd puked, she yells back, "Later!"

We're almost there. I can see the door, but I hafta stop just a second to blow on my hands, cover my aching ears.

She reaches the opening, turns the flashlight back at me. "Hurry up!"

I tuck my chin against the wind, somehow manage to sprint to the door without wiping out. "You so owe me."

She slams me with "as if!" and, as she pulls herself up the stairs, zings me again. "If it weren't for Marvel Girl, you'd still be out there dreaming."

Believe that?

CHAPTER 10

There's a pond down by Thompson's Point that only Libby-town kids know about. You hafta walk the tracks and go through some woods to get to it. I suck at skating, so I've only been there once. Derek let me go with him 'cause all his friends were doing something. When your brother's in sixth grade and you're in third, he don't even want you walking down the street with him, so I was jacked he asked me. Anyway, we get down there and it's all these high school kids: Crab Maxwell, Tim O'Brien, Reggie Staples, some of their friends. I know who they are, for they live in the neighborhood, but soon as I see them, I wanna go home 'cause I'm wicked scared. When Derek asked me to come skating, I figured Deering Oaks, where you can buy hot chocolate when you get cold. Didn't know he meant this place, where you get eaten alive by pricker bushes just to get there and where guys in high school are drinkin' and smokin' and playin' hockey. One look, and going home is what I'm thinking, but Derek's having none of that. He don't care how old they are or how fast they can skate or that we're trespassing on their secret turf. He tells me, *Stop being a titty-baby*, 'cause he didn't walk all the way down there for nothing. Says, *One of 'em's gonna want a butt break sometime.*

I don't want to be a *titty-baby*, but I can't help it; I start bawling—I was just a little kid, whaddaya want? I mean, third grade, what's that? Like, eight? But I put my skates on, 'cause if I didn't, Derek said, *Yuh never comin' with me again.* Back in the day, he could make me do anything. Make me believe anything he said: *This is a free country; they don't own this ice.*

Minute our skates are on, he ditches me. Skates right out there and starts workin' Crab Maxwell so he'll let him play. Pretty impressive—sixth grade, ain't even got a stick, and somehow he weasels his way into being a sub. Classic Derek.

Me, I'm too petrified of getting run over by one of those big guys or nailed by that black puck to go anywhere near 'em. I only dare to wobble around on the crappy section where the cattails and reeds grow right up outta the ice and catch your blades faster than tar. Between diggers, I watch the game, and, even from that far away, I can tell Derek ain't lovin' having to come out each time a break's over or having to wait for someone to want one or how they never pass him the puck, even when he's wide open. Can also tell not all the guys are happy about him being their sub just by the way Reggie won't let him borrow his stick while he's chugging a beer and how Bucktooth Barney gives Derek a cheap shot from behind, probably hoping it'll scare him enough to make him go home.

I'm hoping for that, too, 'cause I'm so cold my snot's turned into icicles and, worse, I gotta take a leak. Though the pond's surrounded by trees and thick bushes, it's fed by the bay, that air off the ocean sharp enough to cut yuh skin, cold enough that I totally believe Derek's story about *the hobo who got frostbite on his wiener and had to have it cut off*, so I don't dare to chance it.

I'm also really over getting tripped by the sticks and bumpy ice in the crappy section. So next time I fall, I'm laying there bawling and wishin' I'd never come when I see something moving in the reeds. There I am, flat on the ice, and it's staring right at me. Freakin' muskrat, size of a toy poodle!

I know I must've screamed, or they wouldn't have stopped their game, but I don't remember doing it. What I do remember, I wish I could forget. How they chase it onto the ice and start clubbing it.

How it squeals only once.

How Derek keeps whacking and whacking even after it's dead.

How he pushes its body across the ice like a hockey puck.

How suddenly everyone's looking at him like he's crazy or a hero—someone definitely good enough to be a sub.

I grab my boots and don't look back. Scramble right through those woods with my skates on. Never even feel the branches that scratch me to shit, that steal the hat right off my head and stab my cheek bad enough for three stitches. Isn't till I get to the tracks, where I stop to put my boots on, that I realize the wet stuff on my face ain't titty-baby tears.

Was never so cold in my life, walking home from there with a crew cut and no hat and my pants frozen stiff with piss. Not even sitting in soaked clothes on a bus with no heat in the middle of a blizzard for forty-five minutes is close. Still, it's cold enough to make me think of that muskrat and what really happened instead of Derek's version, which I wanna believe. Lot easier to pretend he was saving me from getting bit.

"Where the heck they sending that bus from—New York?" asks Cheez-It, who's been yapping the whole time about how her lawyer's gonna sue everybody—the driver, the bus company, the EMTs for not taking her to the hospital for her whiplash, the weathermen who should've known it was gonna snow, the plows for not doing a good enough job, the tractor trailer drivers who think they own the road, and the State of Massachusetts for allowing them to drive like maniacs.

"If she says one more thing," whispers Purplehead, "I'm going to throw her off that snowbank out there so that one of those tractor trailers can run her over."

"Really," I agree.

"Then I'll steal her blanket and pillow," she adds.

We both laugh at that, but Purplehead ain't done; she's on a roll. "O-wen," she says in a raspy voice. "Go bury him in the yard before he stinks up the place."

"*Throw Momma from the Train*," I answer.

"Well, look who just caught on," she tells me.

I'm starting to like this game, her one-liners, her funny voices. Even though she's the reason my toes have morphed into Popsicles, I'm over being mad at her. After the big brouhaha of cops and EMTs checkin' everyone out and leaving with the ones they had to, she'd told me why she took off after she'd puked. *I just lost it, pulled a Mrs. Chase, thought, I'm outta here! But then I got to the top of the snowbank and was, like, No way you can walk home from this place, girlfriend!*

I figure, with what happened to her mom, and seeing all those accidents, it ain't her fault she wigged after that toboggan ride. I mean, look at me: up there like a deer in headlights—talk about nimrods. Better never sign up for the army. Wouldn't be able to trust myself; probably freeze up or start thinking about stuff that didn't even matter. Really, I can picture it, be in that movie war for real, trapped in one of them tanks, Scud missiles explodin' all around me, and I'd waste my last moment on the planet thinking how I wouldn't be able to tell Frankie a new *worst way to die*. Found that out tonight. Still be out there dreaming if it weren't for her. So what if my sneakers got soaked and my feet are still frozen; I owe her. She's freakin' Marvel Girl! Forget Coleen and her blond hair and tool of a brother. There's girls out there way better—even if they got earrings stickin' outta their eyebrows. That's why I sat with her again, though I told Gramp it was 'cause I didn't want to get him all wet.

"They better make sure they get my luggage on that new bus," Cheez-It announces, "that's all I'm saying."

The Suck-Face Couple, sitting right behind her, don't believe that for a second. They get up and move; take the empty seats where Leo and Joey were. We lucked out there—Bawling Baby won her fam a free ride to their aunty's with a cop 'cause one of the EMT guys didn't want her *sitting on a bus with no heat for who knows how long in this storm*. Ask me, he just couldn't take her howling, but hey, who can blame him? Not me. It was torture.

Only ones who went off in an ambulance were the broken

nose B-ball boy and our bus driver, who started having chest pains while he was plantin' flares out there with the truck driver. I feel wicked bad now for yelling at him. Probably gonna have a heart attack on his way to the hospital, and the last thing he'll remember is some little troll telling him, *You're the one that drove us off the road.*

"Got my granddaughter's Christmas present in there, and let me tell you, those ZhuZhu Pets don't run cheap," says Cheez-It, her breath floatin' in the beam of our only light. "So what about that?" she wants to know.

"You'll have to ask about your luggage when the driver gets here," says the cop with the 'tude up front, who's holding his flashlight on us like a gun, protecting us from I'm not sure what—maybe us robbing each other or tryin' to escape outta that ceiling hatch. "That's all I can tell you, ma'am."

Officer Tude's more ticked off about being stuck here than we are. Rather be out arresting people like my brother than babysitting us. About every five minutes, he gets on his walkie-talkie to ask his partner waiting in their cruiser up on the road, probably with the heat freakin' blasting, "Any sign of that bus, yet?"

"I had to go all over town for that Mr. Squiggles one she wanted. She'll play with it all of five minutes, but I can't show up empty-handed."

I hear what Cheez-It's sayin' for I'll be dead meat if I

show up without those Italian sandwiches Ma packed in the cooler for Derek. It's his favorite meal. I promised him, promised I'd get 'em from Amato's. Amato's is the best. Gramp says it's their sour pickles; Ma says it's the bread and the olive oil. Trust me, it's a fact. If you're from Maine, you know it—only place to buy Italians is from one of their stores. Derek loves them, would eat them every day if he could. Told me the crap they call hoagies down there ain't even close.

"I can't believe this," says Purplehead, who's rubbing and breathing on her hands. "I mean, what am I supposed to do if my bus leaves for New York before we get there?"

Good question, 'cause me and Gramp gotta catch the same bus she does, but right now all I can think of is if Ma hadn't asked at Amato's for the oil on the side, the bread would already be nice and soggy. God, I'd give ten bucks for just a bite; can almost smell those green peppers and onions right through the floor, want one so bad. I'd even try eating those nasty black olives Derek loves on his.

"What time's it now, Chappy?"

"Steal yourself a watch," says his friend. "I'm done telling you every two minutes."

"I should have listened to my mother and worn my L. L. Bean coat," admits Purplehead, who's shivering so bad her teeth are clickin' like the Wheel of Fortune. "My father better feel guilty when I die of frostbite. Really, he pays nine hundred dollars for his new son's crib, and he can't even buy me a plane ticket?"

Nine hundred bucks! For a crib? Ask him to buy me a bed, I wanna tell her. "Sounds like he can afford it."

"Don't go there," she warns me. "If my mom had had his lawyer, I'd be sitting in first class on a plane."

I hear her, 'cause if Derek had had a good lawyer, time he'd borrowed that car, he wouldn't have had to wait in juvie till his case got heard. Of course that was Derek's way of looking at it, *borrowed*. But the car's owner, who'd left it parked and running while he popped into a 7-Eleven, and the cops who chased Derek all over Portland till he crashed into a snowplow on West Street, saw it another way—theft of a motor vehicle, driving without a license, and about five other charges, including resisting arrest and drunk driving. *Boys will be boys* and *junior high's such a rough stage* didn't cut it for my parents anymore. Derek's drunken toot around P-town in a *borrowed* car was a real wake-up call for them, made 'em finally face the truth—*he's a head case, he needs help*. And if he'd had a lawyer like the one Purplehead was talkin' about, Derek wouldn't have had to wait, woulda been in Winstonbrook the very next day.

"My father ever wants to see me again, he's coming to

Maine," says Purplehead. "Can't even feel my fingers anymore."

I take my gloves off and give them to her. "Here, put these on."

"You sure?"

"My coat has pockets," I tell her.

"You're the bomb," she says, then asks, "Didn't you have a hat, too?"

"I didn't pay a fortune for a bus ticket to show up without a change of Hanes and no ZhuZhu Pet for my only grandkid. Not when her Nana Moolah bought her a *Dora* Designer Dollhouse. So they better—"

"Jumping Jesus! Someone stick a sock in that piehole!" yells BO, cutting off Cheez-It and crackin' up the boys in the back.

"Sir, that's enough!" It's Officer Tude, and he's all business. "I'm *done* warning you about your language."

Forget you and your flashlight, is what I'm thinking, 'cause everyone on this bus is done. Done freezing, done worrying, done waiting.

And BO's really done 'cause his Dunkin' Donut cup's on empty, and so's the bottle he kept fillin' it up with. "Go ahead! Arrest me! Need a warm place to sleep tonight."

Wish Derek were here—he'd be dying. *Need a warm*

place to sleep tonight—even Cheez-It thinks it's wicked funny. And now we're all on the same page—us against the cop.

Abe Lincoln's clone, who wouldn't move his stuff when I was looking for a seat, says, "Arrest me first. I can't wait any longer." Then he fires up a Marlboro.

Next thing you know, people are breaking out smokes and sharin' Bics. I'm thinking that cop better call in the Sentinels 'cause he's got a mutant nest on his hands. Even Gramp heads up back with a stogie, asking, "This the smoking section?"

"It is now," says Abe, and, moving his stuff, tells Gramp, "Have a seat, friend."

"Been trying to quit," admits Cheez-It in between drags. "Can't smoke in their house. They make me go outside on the sidewalk like a criminal."

I look back at the cop, expecting trouble, but he don't say a thing.

Guess he's smarter than I thought.

CHAPTER 11

With Gramp's arm across my shoulders and my head just about wedged in his armpit, I can feel his whole body shaking as me and his new best bud help him toward the snowbank. *Almost there!* I wanna tell him, but I'm too tired, and the wind trying to knock me over is whistling so loud Gramp won't hear me anyway.

We were the first ones off the bus, but everyone's passed us. Suitcase Man flew by so fast I don't think his feet even broke snow. Purplehead stuck with us long enough to know she couldn't help—'bout ten seconds.

Each time Gramp had to stop for a rest, it was someone else. The Suck-Face Couple.

Others I never noticed enough to name.

Tude, his partner, and our new bus driver carrying Cheez-It like the Pope.

Now BO—who the B-ball boys dragged by on someone's coat as if it were a sled—has even made it over the bank.

So when Gramp holds up his hand for another rest, I feel like crying 'cause I wanna be on that new bus gettin' warm like everybody else.

Abe Lincoln does, too.

Soon as Gramp lifts his hand, Abe ducks away from him, then takes off: starts scrambling up the snowbank like a yeti.

I can't believe it. Can't freakin' believe it!

But the new weight on my shoulders and my left leg sinking deeper tell me it's true. And suddenly, I don't care about nothin' but getting ahold of that sock that's worked its way off my heel and morphed into a killer rock beneath my foot. But that means letting go of Gramp, and I can't do that; he might fall, might hurt himself, might drop that freakin' thermos he wouldn't leave on the bus, even though the driver told him to.

We only make it a couple of steps before a flashlight comes bobbing down the snowbank. It's the cop, and he's got the B-ball boys with him. Soon as they get Gramp, I take care of that sock that's been cuttin' into my skin like broken glass.

CHAPTER 12

Back in the day, when we used to be happy, one of Ma's favorite stories was how she met my dad. If she had more than one beer at a neighborhood barbecue, all the mothers would get the replay. Didn't bother them, though, for Ma always threw in some new thing no one had heard before about her and Dad's summers at the lake.

Even givin' the short version, there's things you gotta know. Like, my grandparents on my dad's side, who live in Connecticut and have nothing to do with us, are loaded. No joke, they got a camp on Little Sebago that's bigger than the house we used to own. I was too little to remember ever going there, but I've seen pictures. It's wicked nice. Right outta some magazine—you know, got the pine trees, the huge deck, stone stairs that take you right down to the water. It's impressive. I'm serious. They got everything—beach, dock, big deluxe boat.

Anyway, they also used to own a little camp right next to theirs that Gramp rented for a week every year while Ma and my uncles were growin' up. My uncles say it wasn't too shiny, but that's why they loved it. *Wasn't nothing us kids could wreck, and we could bring the dog.* From listening to them a million times, I know it had *a one-man bathroom and a kitchen not much bigger*, that they *had to put out the pots and pans when it rained because only thing holding the roof together was pine needles and mouse turd*, that in the living room there was a *GIANT* stone fireplace, and it was the *only thing still standing when the place burned down.*

But when Ma's describing *upta camp*, she never mentions those things. Listening to her, you'd think they rented a palace, 'cause *it was right on the water and had a screened-in porch.* She'd make you wish you could go there, way she'd talk about canoeing and fishin' and *staying up all night telling ghost stories in front of the fire*, make you wanna see those *unbelievable sunsets* and *killer thunderstorms* and have a camp you could *talk and dream about all winter.* So, no matter how many times those mothers heard about Ma meetin' Dad when they were *both in diapers,* and how by junior high they were *just like the loons, mates for life*, the mothers never complained, and neither did I.

But we haven't been to a barbecue for a long time. Now the only story Ma tells about *upta camp* starts with how Dad's parents never wanted him to marry *that renter's daughter*, how they'd told him he was *throwing his life away* when he moved up to Maine, how they hadn't *paid for private schools for him to go to SMVTI and become an electrician*. If she's really wound up, Ma throws in *married for eighteen years, and they still don't have the decency to call me by my real name. I'm "that wife of his" or "the mother."* I know it pretty much by heart, always ends with *last time I stepped foot on that property was the day his father said, "If you'd listened to me, you could've been somebody."*

Still, every once in a while, when she's on the phone with one of my uncles and don't know I'm spying, she'll say somethin' I never heard. Like, I never knew my dad opens and closes up my grandparents' camp for them every year, that he checks on it in the winter, that he redid the electrical out of his own pocket. To me, their camp was like their house in Connecticut, a place we never went to. Just figured Dad never went there, either. I already knew that *in all the years we've been married, he never asked his father for a red cent*, but I didn't know Dad asked Grandfather Phil to lend him the money for a lawyer to get Derek outta juvie, and how *it killed him to do that, and killed him even more when that bastard said no.*

That's what's going through my brain while we're thawing out on the new bus and drivin' into Boston. Thinkin' how if it'd been Grandfather Pill with me instead of Gramp, I woulda took off like Abe Lincoln and let him break his freakin' neck. I mean, what's up with that? Got all that money and won't even help his own son? Derek would be dead or doing time in Windham if our dad was like that. He'd do anything for us kids. And Gramp, he'd do anything, too. Might not be able to loan my parents money to pay the lawyer and medical bills, but we'd be sleeping in the Preble Street Shelter if it weren't for him.

"You warmin' up, Gramp?" I ask, turning away from the window and blur of fast food restaurants.

"Glad I kept my thermos," he tells me, holding up its cup. "Coffee's still hot. That's the thing about a Stanley, Zach, it's a hundred percent stainless steel with vacuum insulation. Best there is. If you take care of it, it'll last forever. Your gram got me this for Christmas the year your uncle Curly was born; that's how durable they are."

Know why Gramp wouldn't leave it behind now, and it ain't 'cause it's made of stainless steel. "I 'member the Etch-A-Sketch she bought me," I tell him. "That was awesome."

"Your brother Derek used to run her ragged, but she loved looking after you. All she had to do was give you a boxa crayons and some paper, and you'd be happy as a clam. She called you her little Rockwell. She saved every dang picture, even the ones you drew of her when she went bald, which, to be honest, I wasn't too pleased about."

Inappropriate humor—even back then?

"They're kicking around in a box somewhere down cellar. She made me promise that I wouldn't throw them away."

"She used to hang 'em on the fridge with alphabet magnets. Used to say when I was famous, they'd be worth a lot of money." Made me feel like I was all that and a bag of chips.

Out the window it's an ocean of red taillights and a million lanes of cars honking and cuttin' in front of each other— one oil truck's so close to us, I could reach out and pick the guy's nose. Who'd wanna live here?

As the bridge we're winding our way around heads past Boston Gardens, the boys in the back give up a weak "yahoo," as if they don't give a rip no more.

Sucks to be them.

Like their face paint, the fun's already ruined.

Know the feeling. Last day of school, seventh grade— perfect example. Everyone's going to Funtown, right? It's a given. A tradition. It's all kids talk about 'cause, for most of them, it's the first time their parents don't go with, just give 'em a ride. That's the beauty of it, no parents. Six hours of hangin' with half the school, going on rides, eating anything yuh want. Plus the slim possibility of making out with Coleen in the Haunted House. I saved for weeks. Had it all arranged: Frankie's mom was gonna drop us off, Tony's dad pick us up. Big day comes—freakin' pours out. Story of my life.

"Don't know what ever happened to that Etch-A-Sketch," I tell Gramp as we enter a tunnel with white walls almost as blinding as the blizzard it's protecting us from. "Probably went to Goodwill during one of Ma's cleanin' campaigns."

"That's probably where my knife sharpener ended up when she rearranged my kitchen," Gramp agrees. "I still can't get used to having the silverware in that other drawer."

Don't like this tunnel. Gives me the elevator heebies—that trapped, stuck-between-floors, building's-on-fire, can't-escape feelin' that always makes me sick to my stomach. Ever get that? People in those cars flyin' by us know what I'm talking about—let's get outta here or die tryin' is the way they're driving. No way I could live in this city. Soon as I saw those tall buildings all crammed together from that pretzel of a bridge I was certain of that—I'd spend my whole life walking up and down stairs.

How long can this tunnel be? I'm wondering that when

everyone starts slammin' on their brakes, the screeching sound echoing off the walls, giving me nightmare shivers.

In a nanosecond, we go from flyin' to wheels barely moving. Now we're stuck in this death trap—it's a scene right outta *X-Men*, perfect location for a mutant ambush. Can already see the frame: Professor Xavier, wearin' his Cerebro system, psychic abilities mag'd to the max, warning, "Get outta there ASAP, or you'll die from the nuclear exhaust!"

Could bust out a window with Gramp's Stanley.

Could escape out the hatch.

But it's all cars—no sidewalks, no place to run.

Got that hot dog stuck in my throat all over again, barely able to whisper to Gramp, "Why ain't we movin'?"

He shrugs like it's no big deal. "Time of day. Snowstorm. Celtics are playing. Take your choice."

I stare out the window at the bumper-to-bumper cars beside us, then at the curve blockin' the view of what's ahead. Only choice I got's to believe him. Like when he told me, *Be mad all you want, Zach, but trust me on this: You can't hate your parents for getting him help the only way they could.*

I know he's right, saw what they went through, one doctor after another, one guess after another, one test after another, this med, that med, you name it, Derek was on it at some time. Ma kept saying, *Those quacks don't know what they're doing*, but when yuh got a kid that can lie as good as Derek, I think she's lucky they were trying to guess at all. I mean who do you believe if you're the doctor? The kid who can charm a bum outta their last penny or the mother who's crying and yelling, *I'm sick of this medical merry-go-round, I want answers*? That's what happened the one and only time I got stuck going to one of those nightmare appointments, which were a battle for Ma to drag Derek to. I'm sure that doctor was some glad to see us exit his office. Pretty sure he was thinking it was Ma who had the problem and not Derek, too. Thing is, if he'd heard what Derek said on the ride home and saw him put his fist through the garage window when we got there, that doctor mighta changed his mind.

Long story short, a year and a half after Derek stole a car from the 7-Eleven parking lot 'cause *it was too far to walk home*, Ma finally got her answer—bipolar.

CHAPTER 13

Soon as we get to South Station, we get the bad news—our bus to New York's canceled; next one won't be leaving till the storm lets up. Merry freakin' Christmas.

While Gramp's waiting in line for answers, Purplehead, who's stickin' to me like dog hair, whispers, "I don't think we're in Kansas anymore."

Cracks me up; she's so right. The place is huge, and everywhere yuh look are people—from just born to just about dead, street bum to briefcase, some races I don't even know.

"What's up with the guys in the robes?" I ask.

"Muslims," answers Purplehead. "If my uncle Mickey were here, he'd say, 'There goes the neighborhood.' He's such a backwoods bigot. This place would freak him out."

Know I've heard the word but forget what it means. "Bigot?"

I'm regretting I asked before she even answers. "Someone who's prejudiced," she says in her teacher voice. "You know, anti everything and anybody who doesn't think or act or look like they do."

I'm thinking, *Way to go, dipwad,* 'cause soon as she says *prejudiced* I remember what it means. So now she not only knows I'm a basketball star, but I'm freakin' stupid, too.

"If you Google it," says Purplehead, "you'll see a picture of my uncle. He should be banned from the public. He's so ignorant, he thinks my cousin Sam can be cured of being gay; he tells him all he needs is the right woman."

I give a fake laugh; it's all I got, for now she's got me wondering if maybe I'm a bigot. I mean, seriously, some of these people look pretty freaky to me. Like, wouldn't want that old guy with the long beard livin' in my neighborhood. Tell me he ain't a child molester, probably got a puppy under that big coat and just waitin' for a lost kid. And the man by the pole who's built like a NFL linebacker—be lying if I told yuh I wasn't scared of him. Not sure if it's that he's black or that he could snap me in half like a chicken bone or those pink boots he's wearing, but he's definitely pushin' my *stranger-danger* button. Now there's a thought cloud that'd never fly in the *Roundtable*; they'd probably kick me outta school for a *hate crime*, say I was a bigot and a racist all rolled in one. Thing is, looking around here, maybe I am and just never knew it till now. I mean, if I were here with Derek, the stuff I'm thinking he'd be saying out loud, and we'd be laughing about it. Can hear him now: *Don't be bending over in front of that guy.* So, is that sick? To think like that? Does it mean I'm gettin' what Derek's got?

I look over at Gramp, who's finally made it to the counter, and suddenly I'm wondering what people in this United Nations of a bus station might be thinking of him—old-fart white guy? That make them bad? That make them not normal? Probably think the same thing if I didn't know him. Freakin' Purplehead, what does she know? Still, I tell her, "My best friend's black."

"So?" she asks, like she don't get what I'm saying.

"So I didn't want you to think I'm like your uncle."

"I know that," she answers. "You never would've sat with me if you were."

"It's not like I had a choice," I point out.

She smiles like she's telling me a secret, says, "You did the second time."

You'd think that'd make me feel better, but it don't. Makes me feel like a skid for using Frankie, you know, using his being black to make me look like a saint. How low-rent is that? Now I know how Judas felt sellin' out his BFF. Still, wouldn't hang myself for it, wouldn't off myself with a box cutter—that's a good sign, right?

'Sides, Frankie do the same as me if he was standing here with a gorgeous girl talking about her bigot uncle. He'd tell her, "My best friend's white," to prove he ain't prejudiced: be a fool not to—we're talking a high school sophomore with for-real boobs wearin' a black leather jacket and low-rider jeans. Know what I'm saying? She could mess up anybody's head. I'm gettin' off just standing here pretending I'm her boyfriend.

Gramp's face is all red and not looking happy when he walks over to us. "I waited in that long line for nothing," he tells us. "She didn't even know our bus went off the road."

"What about our luggage?" Purplehead asks him.

"She said she'd try to find out when things settle down. I'll check back later."

For me that means no dry socks. No Amato's Italian.

For Purplehead it's worse. "My Demonias are in there," she says, her face turning puke white. "It took two paychecks to buy them."

I know she works weekends at a movie theater but don't got a clue what Demonias are. Must be something really important, though, 'cause she looks down at her feet and bursts into tears.

Feel wicked bad for her, but whadda you do? Look away so she don't feel embarrassed? Give her a hug?

Ix-nay on the hug. No can do. Not in front of Gramp and all these people. Not sure I could do that if it were only her and me, so I just stand there like an idiot and watch Gramp put his arm around her shoulder.

"It's okay, dear," he says, giving her a little squeeze. "You're just tired."

Way to show me up, Gramp! Can't pretend she's my girl-friend now!

"Try to look on the bright side," he tells her. "We're all right. We didn't have to go to the hospital like that poor boy or the driver. That's what's important."

"I'm sorry," says Purplehead, rubbing the tears from her face like a little kid. "That was so stupid. I'm such a wa-wa baby. I can't help it. It just happens. I should come with a warning." She starts laughing, tells Gramp, "Sad movie? They make me sit by myself."

"I understand completely," says Gramp. "My wife used to cry watching *Little House on the Prairie*. She could never leave the house without a handkerchief."

I don't get why that's funny, but they both laugh. Then Gramp takes his arm off her shoulder, pats her on the back, says, "You stick with us. We'll take care of you."

"Thanks," she tells him. "I'm okay now. Really." She wipes beneath her eyes with two fingertips, says, "I just want to find a bathroom; my face must be a mess."

Staring at the black smudges on her cheeks, at the lashes that are still wet and shiny, I wonder if I'm ever gonna understand girls.

"I know I could use a restroom," says Gramp, then he looks at me.

"Sounds like a plan," I tell him, 'cause I've been holding this Mountain Dew piss since Portsmouth.

In the men's room, there's a bum with his shirt off taking a cat bath in the sink and another bum taking a nap on the floor, but when I come outta the stall, I see something even scarier—Gramp standing there in his bare feet and underwear holding his pants under the hand dryer. You were me, wouldn't you pretend you didn't know him?

I don't even stop to wash my hands, book right outta there before he spots me. But once I'm safe, I start gettin' scared for him, yuh know? Start thinking all kinds of things, like, What if those bums in there mug him and take his wallet? Or what if some little kid tells his parents there's a man in the bathroom with no pants on?

So I go back in there to protect Gramp from the bums and the cops who'll arrest him for being a perv, and know what he tells me? "Take your pants off, Zach, and dry them. You don't want to be sitting around here for hours in wet clothes; you'll catch pneumonia."

Like I'm mental enough to do that—and he's the one who likes to say, *Derek didn't get that from my side of the family.*

I tell him I'm okay, my jeans are almost dry, that the girl's already outside waiting for us. I leave again, hoping the last lie will hurry him up. There's no sign of Purplehead, so I guard the entrance of the men's room, giving people going in a heads-up: "Guy in there dryin' his pants ain't a pervert; he's my grandfather." Some of them laugh. Most don't even slow down enough to listen. One says, "Sorry, kid, don't have any change."

Got any idea how long it takes to dry a pair of pant legs and some socks on one of them hand dryers? Forever! Each time I hear Gramp pound that sucker when it stops, the madder I get. Feels like the night Derek ditched me at the Sea Dogs game. He'd bought tickets for my birthday, and Ma was so happy he'd done something like that, she let him take me—which was huge, 'cause he'd just gotten outta Winston-brook. I was wicked stoked about going, and for the first three innings, it was awesome: Derek totally in *good mood mode* and crackin' me up about the players and people in the crowd.

But then he ran into a couple of guys he knew while we were buying hot dogs and that was the end of that good time. Said he was gonna sit with 'em for a few minutes and meet me back at the seats. Never did. Kept searching for his face in the crowd, kept going back to the hot dog stand between innings, kept looking at that empty seat beside me, worried something mighta happened to him one minute, wantin' to kill him the next 'cause he's probably off somewhere gettin' drunk.

Bottom of the seventh, it starts raining; by the top of the ninth, only me and the die-hards are still in the stands. I'm miserable but can't leave in case he shows up. Can't even re-member who won the game but know it got over about eleven. I waited outside the stadium till all the people came out—no Derek. Walk home knowing he ain't gonna be there and that I'm stuck with having to tell Ma and Dad the truth. Happy Birthday, Zach.

That's the merry memory in my brain when Gramp finally comes out, smiling and bragging, "I'm a whole new man. My feet are warm as toast."

"'Bout time," I bark at him.

"What's with you?" he asks.

"You're the one who's supposed to be lookin' out for me!" I yell at him and don't give a rip people are watching. "That wasn't too smart, Gramp. Those bums in there coulda mugged you."

His smile's history. "I never even gave it a thought," he says. "But you're right. So don't you ever do what I just did. Okay, Zach?"

I'm not that stupid. "Don't worry, I won't."

"Good. Good." He pats me on the shoulder, says, "I'm sorry if I scared you, son. Sometimes your gramp forgets he's an old man."

"It's okay," I tell him, even though it's not.

"And, Zach, it's probably best if we didn't mention this to your mother. You know how she can get. She won't let me take you anywhere again."

He's got that right—just ask Derek.

"Sorry it took me so long," says Purplehead, whose make-up's back in place, black lipstick and all. "I needed to let my dad know about our bus and touch base with my mom."

"Good idea," says Gramp, then he takes out his wallet and hands me a twenty. "Why don't you two go upstairs and get yourselves something to eat? I'll go find a pay phone and call home, let them know we're all right."

"Pay phone?" asks Purplehead.

Gramp laughs, says, "I know they're on the endangered list, but I don't think they're extinct yet."

"Would you like to use my cell?" offers Purplehead, already diggin' into her skull bag.

"Oh, no, no," Gramp tells her. "Thank you, dear, but I wouldn't even know how to operate one of those contraptions."

"You need to get with the times," she tells him.

He smiles, says, "Not until I have to. I'm sure they still have a few pay phones around here for old fogies like me."

After seeing Gramp in his baggy Fruit of the Looms in the men's room, I'm not sure I should let him loose on his own. "That's okay, Gramp, we'll go with you."

He tilts his head at me then laughs like he just heard a good joke. "He thinks he's my mother now," he tells Purplehead.

Ask him why, I wanna tell her, but what comes out is "Somebody's gotta be."

He gives me a fake knuckle punch on the arm. "I'll be fine, wise guy," he says, the blue eyes beneath those *albino caterpillars* letting me know he's serious, he's still my grandfather, he doesn't need a babysitter—all that in one look.

"Okay, okay," I tell him, but he ain't fooling me. He just wants to ditch us 'cause he's havin' a nic fit and making that call's a perfect excuse. But I ain't complaining—I'll take the twenty bucks.

"I'll meet you up there when I'm done," says Gramp, already scoutin' for the nearest exit.

"Just look for my hair," Purplehead tells him. "I'm easy to find."

"Tell Ma I said hi." I shove the bill in my pocket, and we head toward the escalator and the smell of French fries.

"You kids stay together," Gramp calls after us.

I turn and give him a warnin' of my own: "Don't tell her our bus went off the road!"

Though I can't see him good with all the people, I hear his laugh. Hear him answer, "Yes, Mother!"

CHAPTER 14

Like I said, if you're not bleeding in the ER, or having a baby or a heart attack, you're last on the list. It's somethin' we already know, but we take Derek in anyway 'cause he hasn't eaten or gotten outta bed or swore at us for days. I mean, this time's different; he's really out of it, a total zombie. He doesn't even put up a fight about going and that's a major red flag. Ma thinks it's the medication *that new doctor, who can't even speak English* put Derek on, but she can't get ahold of him 'cause it's a weekend and *he's probably off somewhere on his yacht.* She's wild. They waited four months just to see the guy and had to pay up front 'cause he don't deal with insurance, which also means our insurance don't gotta pay for the crap that's turned my brother into a voidoid, so Ma had to shell out at the pharmacy, too. Can you follow that? Not even sure I got it right, and I listened to it over and over, whole ride to the hospital. What I do know for sure is my brother's so blazed he can't even tell yuh his name and—*cha-ching, cha-ching*—cost Ma 264 bucks.

Anyway, it's a full moon and a Saturday night, and the place's so packed they got stretchers in the hall. It's a wicked zoo—drunks with broken jaws, gruntin' pregnant mothers, people hackin' up their lungs, some guy puking his guts out in a wastebasket—it just keeps coming through the front door. Plus we keep hearing the sirens, which means there's an ambulance bringing in something worse through the back door, so we're gonna wait forever. I remember thinking at one point, *I don't blame them*—the people who work there. I mean, Derek's slouched in a chair, staring off into la-la land, not makin' a sound, and in comes a guy who's all bent over he's in so much pain, and he's moaning about blood in his urine and a stone he can't pass—tell me you wouldn't take him over my brother. Know what I'm saying? Felt like jumping up and yelling, "Get that man a doctor 'fore he dies!"

Ask me, they should have a place where people like Derek can go. That way he'd only get bumped by a mental case worse off than he is, wouldn't hafta sit around for hours, wouldn't hafta see and hear and smell gross stuff that'd wig him out even more. Seriously, you wanna know what hell's like, spend a few hours in that waitin' room next to a guy with rank diarrhea, watching a drunk with two black eyes and a busted jaw drool blood on a towel and listening to some lady without a tooth in her head yap about the pus coming outta her privates. Short version—thirteen hours later, my butt's so numb I can't feel it, Dad's head is ready to explode, and Ma says, "Let's go home."

So having to wait around South Station's a piece of cake for me. We set up camp on a bench near one of the spaceship-looking silver columns and take turns guarding our spot against the bums and stranded people like us. When Gramp gets back from having a cigar, or buying another coffee, or checking on our luggage, whatever, me and Purplehead cruise. We check out everything—the Celtics/Bruins/Red Sox cart, food court, shops, the trains. We each buy a pair of socks and trash our wet ones. Gramp's right: Having dry feet makes yuh a whole new man.

At first, Gramp wants us to check back with him every fifteen minutes, but after a while he don't care if we're gone thirty or forty-five, for he's made friends with an old guy and his wife from Virginia, who are camped out on the same bench with us. Seriously, could drop Gramp in the middle of a desert, and he'd find someone to talk to and then know a friend of theirs or some relative. It's a relief he's got buds to hang with 'cause me and Purplehead are havin' a blast together going off on our own. Before long, we know where the cleanest and fastest bathrooms are, what places sell the cheapest eats and drinks, and the best windows to check on the snow. Hall with the huge windows at the entryway to Atlantic Avenue is our fave. Don't got any benches and it's colder, but there's no people 'cept the ones coming in or leaving. The best things are it's quieter and darker. Great place to talk and watch the snow fallin' on Chinatown, or out the other three big windows near the elevator, watch the trains.

The more I learn about Purplehead, the more I like her— she checks change slots on vending machines for money, loves animals so much she don't eat meat, can whistle with two fingers. Who wouldn't like her? Plus she's wicked funny. No lie, we're walkin' past the Suck-Face Couple, camped by the big clock and just about doing it with their clothes on, and she tells them, "Rent a room—you're making me jealous." That's what I'm talkin' about—got her own sense of *inappropriate humor*. Even they cracked up.

Next time we check in, the two of us guard Gramp's Stanley and his Virginia Friends' suitcases while they go to *the real restaurant*, which ain't on the cheap eats and drinks list. Bench space is primo, and if you don't defend it, people will move right in on yuh. Let 'em get one butt-cheek on your bench, their whole fam will be sitting there before you know it. To protect our turf from invaders of the rude and sneaky kind, we use the couple's luggage, my backpack, the Stanley, our bodies. When we're done building our barricade, Purplehead says, "No one, and I mean no one, comes into our house and pushes us around."

"Rudy! Rudy! Rudy!" I chant, like the crowd in the movie.

"Isn't that awesome?" she asks, those brown eyes starting to dance. "Best time to catch it: fall, early on a Sunday morning. I watch *Rudy* just about every time it comes on."

When we used to have cable, I did, too, but instead of telling her that, I remind her, "Thought you didn't like jocks?"

"I don't, but he isn't typical; he's the underdog. Favorite part?" she demands.

"When he sacks the quarterback," I tell her. "And havin' his dad there to see 'im do it."

"Not!" she fires back. "It's when they carry him off the field. Once I cried so hard I got the hiccups."

After what she'd told Gramp about her crying problem, "That's a given."

She punches me in the arm, tells me, "Don't be mean."

I grab her wrist so the fist with its snake ring can't nail me again, ask, "What are Demonias, anyway?"

She tilts her head back, and the sound of that real laugh

and the view of her slender neck fringed with feathery purple hair is so beautiful, I forget what I just asked.

Even when she turns her face toward me and chokes out the word *boots,* it don't register.

"Boots?" I ask, still confused.

She loses it. She's laughing so hard she's makin' snort noises, which gets me going, then neither one of us can stop for now we're laughing at each other's laugh. We're dying, and the people shootin' us dirty looks make it even funnier. It's so hilarious it's torture. My stomach muscles are spazzin', and the cramps hurt so bad I gotta bend over to breathe. I raise a hand in defeat, beg in a whisper, "No more." And just when I think we got a truce, she whispers back, "Boots," and that kills us all over again.

Finally Purplehead, who's gagging for air, can't take it anymore. She shoves the old lady's pink suitcase off the bench and lies down on her back. Her coat's flapped open and seeing those lovely sandcastles rising and fallin' as she tries to catch her breath sends a shiver through me like gettin' in a hot tub after swimming in a pool.

Feeling faint, I knock the old guy's suitcase off the bench and lay down, too. "Good idea," I tell her. "Thought I was gonna pass out."

"I know," she pants. "I'm exhausted."

Although we're lying on the bench with our bodies in the

opposite direction, the top of our heads are almost touching, and for just a second, Ma's warnin' about bugs floats through my brain. Probably could catch something worse from this bench with all the butts that have sat on it, but I'm too tired to move, and it feels so good to lie down.

The first thing I noticed when we got here was the ceiling, and as I stare up at its awesome design, it still blows me away. Whoever thought up that glass and steel in 3-D is someone I wanna meet. "Isn't that wicked cool? It makes me feel like I'm starin' out through an eyeball."

"The spindles remind me of pinwheels," she answers.

"Be even cooler in the daytime with light comin' through the glass," I point out, trying to imagine it.

"Definitely," she agrees. "But I hope we're not here long enough to see it."

"Me, too," I tell her.

Still, in a weird way, I don't want this to be over, either. I mean, yesterday, I woulda been petrified if you told me I had to hang out with a girl in a place like this, but that's the thing: Purplehead's kinda like hangin' out with Frankie. Really, you shoulda seen us laughing over those *Far Side* cards. And she's the one who started the spitball war, had a pile of ammunition rolled up before I even knew what she was up to. Used her straw like a freakin' dart blower!

Don't know about you, but it's totally new territory for me, thinkin' a girl could be a friend you'd actually wanna hang with. Never thought of that happening, only thing on my radar was making out with them or dreaming about doing more. So even though it feels kinda strange, I ain't lying when I tell her, "Too bad you don't live in Portland. We'd have a wicked good time at Bull Moose and Newbury Comics."

When Gramp and Virginia Friends finally come back, I can tell he got in his nightly shot of Captain Morgan, maybe even two, for he shells out another twenty and says, "Buy yourselves some souvenirs, and on your way back, fill this up with coffee."

I take the Stanley, and me and Purplehead cruise. The place is deserted. The only ones left are people stuck like us and the bums, even the last wave of Celtics fans that came through about an hour ago have caught their trains and disappeared. Don't hafta walk far to know we won't be buying any souvenirs. Be lucky to score Gramp's coffee and some sodas 'cause the couple of fast food joints still open won't be for long. Can tell just by the way their workers are banging things around and washing down counters they wanna get the hell outta Busland.

"We'd better get the coffee 'fore we hit the bathrooms," I tell her.

We're waiting for the cheesed-off schmo behind the counter to fill our order, when we hear a ruckus behind us.

I turn around to see what's happening, and there's this dude in the middle of the food court yelling at people. What's weird, he ain't one of the bums. Looks like a college kid, short hair, nice clothes—someone normal.

Pointing at a couple camped at one of the tables, he hollers, "And you!" Then he starts spinning in a circle, arm out straight, finger aiming at people, thumb pumpin' an imaginary trigger. "And you! And you! And you!"

People flinch like his words are real bullets, but their fear's somethin' I'm used to, somethin' I live with. He's Derek, but he's not.

A second later, he's jumping up and down like a pogo stick. "Barack Obama!" he yells. "*O! B! A! M! A! O! B! A! M! A! O! B! A! M! A!*"

Then he drops to his knees, curls into a ball, arms covering his head like he's expecting an explosion or a kick. Even before he starts to groan, I'm moving toward him.

"Don't," says Purplehead, and that mother-teacher voice almost stops me.

What does stop me are the cops. They've come outta the woodwork. Three, four appear outta nowhere. It's unreal how quick there's a circle of blue around him. One cop does the talking; another pats him down for weapons; two stand guard. It's impressive—these guys know what they're doing.

When they help him up, he's a different person. You can

tell by the way he brushes himself off, the tone of his voice. "I'm sorry if I frightened anyone," he tells the cops. "I don't know what happened. It must have been a traumatic event in my life, but I feel better now."

As suddenly as it happened, he's gone, whisked away. Like the cop who stays behind tells us, "Show's over."

Returning to the counter to pay and collect our drinks, Purplehead says, "That was scary."

"Welcome to my life," I tell her. "Coulda been my brother." I hand the twenty to the guy who just wants to go home and is lucky he can.

CHAPTER 15

One of the doctors at Winstonbrook told Ma that finding the right medication and the right doses for kids like Derek is an art 'cause what may work for one patient might not for another. Plus, some patients might have other things going on as well, so it can take a while to get the right combo and fine-tune how much. Took a few go-arounds to find what worked best for Derek, and once he was stabilized, it was like havin' my old brother back. Trouble is, way I look at it, the problem with Derek ain't that he's bipolar, it's that he don't wanna believe he's got it, don't wanna believe that someone who can make anyone laugh, that tough kid who ain't afraid of nobody or nothin' and who's God's gift to women might have somethin' wrong with him like a chemical imbalance in his brain. Soon as he'd feel like his old self, he'd quit taking his medication and go back to his own choice of meds— partying, gettin' wasted, taking off for days, Dad driving around P-town in the middle of the night looking for him. So we'd be right back in the ER 'cause he'd be even worse, right back at Winstonbrook startin' all over again. Like Dad told one doctor, *What am I supposed to do, tie him down and shove the medication down his throat?*

That's why when I saw that Obama kid lose it back there in the food court, my first thought was *he's off his meds.*

"Ready?" asks Purplehead, coming out of the girls' room.

I hand over her soda, say, "More than ready."

We go to our spot to chill, and as soon as we sit down on the floor by the windows, the handful of bums still left in the building file past us luggin' all their worldly goods. The cop herding 'em toward the stairs acts like he knows them, tells the guy wearing three coats, who kinda looks like Beast, "No messing around, Danny, you get in the van with Father Mike tonight. Too much paperwork if we find you frozen in a Dumpster."

With a look of horror on her face, Purplehead whispers, "He's heartless."

But the bums think it's funny. They're laughing about it as

they start clomping down the stairs, and when one says, "For a pack of Camels, Harry, I'll sleep anywhere you want," their laughter's even louder.

I press my face against the window and look down, watch for them to come out of the building. When I'd read the sign hours ago, I'd thought it was a good thing they kick you outta here if you don't got a ticket when they lock the doors at midnight. But after seeing that homeless army trudge by, I'm both mad and sorry. Makes me think, *Least Derek ain't sleepin' in a Dumpster*. Makes me promise he never will.

Outside the snow has let up, can barely see it falling in the glow of those old-fashioned streetlights or the headlights of the big black passenger van. Not sure what the cop's handing out to the bums as they line up and start climbing in: cigarettes?

Rummaging through her bag, Purplehead asks, "Do you have your ticket on you?"

"No," I tell her, watching the cop wave off the leaving van.

"Think we should go back to your grandfather?" she asks, a hint of panic in her voice.

"Probably. But I'm not gonna. We just got here."

Down below, we hear the cop close the door, then the sound of his stamping feet echoes up the stairwell.

"We can go to the other windows," she says, ready to bolt.

But I'm burnt: ain't playing hide-'n'-seek with no one. "Chill," I tell her. "He ain't gonna bother us."

And he don't. Hardly gives us a glance when he walks by, though Purplehead has her ticket out all ready to show him.

I pick up my soda and take a drink. "Toldja."

"Aren't you smart."

The sarcastic way she says it makes me laugh. "I'm a jock-hole basketball star," I remind her. "Whadja expect?"

"You're not the one he'd want to strip-search for drugs," she points out. "People take one look at me and think, Bet she has a couple of fatties in her pocketbook."

"Do you?"

She slugs me. "See?!"

I raise my arm to block any more punches. "Inappropriate humor," I tell her. "It's like your crying—I can't help it."

She laughs, then rests her head back against the window. "And I thought you were so nice."

"Guess you're really gettin' to know me."

"Speaking of that," she says, turning to look at me, "what did you mean back there when you said that kid could have been your brother?"

Usually around girls I go brain-dead, don't got a clue what to talk about. Really, I'm so pathetic, the night I walked Coleen home I had CliffsNotes in my jacket of things to say if

I froze up. But don't need no notes with Purplehead. I tell her the truth. Tell her what I got hiding in New Jersey. Tell her about Derek, how it's good he's in a place that can make him take his meds and go to therapy, a place he can stay long enough to stay better.

Maybe it's everything we been through or 'cause I don't even know her name, but I feel so safe it's easy. And once I start, stories about Derek fly right outta me, mostly funny ones, but one or two of the bad, and when she tells me, "That must be really hard for you," I almost start bawling.

Instead, I clear my throat and tell her, "Sorry to unload on you."

"Hey, I told you about Katherine, about the baby," she points out, those brown eyes lockin' on mine.

I'm not sure if I kiss her or if she kisses me. It just happens.

CHAPTER 16

Walking outta the hospital, the night Ma gave up waiting in the ER, an ambulance came screaming into the parking lot. Knowing whoever was in the back of that flashin' wagon was gonna be seen el pronto, I said something stupid. Said, "Next time just call an ambulance."

And the next night when Derek tried to off himself with the box cutter, we had to. That's not one of the stories I tell Purplehead, but it's one I live with and dream about. Don't matter what my parents say or what I'd like to believe or blame, deep down I know it was my fault.

When we go back to check in with Gramp, it's like he knows what we've been up to 'cause he says, "Where have you two lovebirds been? I was ready to send out a posse."

"Blame me," says Purplehead, plantin' herself down next to Gramp. "I'm corrupting him."

Gramp's *albino caterpillars* spring to life as he laughs. "I love this girl," he tells me when I hand over the Stanley.

"I know," I answer. "She speaks the language."

CHAPTER 17

The snow quits for good around two in the morning, and the first bus out for New York leaves about four. We're on it, but our luggage ain't. Gramp says by the time it catches up with us, we'll be back in Maine, so looks like Derek won't be gettin' his Italian sandwiches, and me and Gramp will be wearing the same outfit for a couple of days. Thing is, that don't even seem important anymore, seems dumb thinking it ever was. Even Purplehead, who seven, eight hours ago was bawling about her boots, don't give a rip. She's lookin' on the bright side; told us, "My dad will just have to buy me some new clothes. Too bad, so sad."

Miniature Man, our new bus driver, is hilarious—about

as tall as a third-grader and still learning English. Tells us in a wicked heavy accent, which Gramp says is Russian, "Any alcohol or smoking you'll be executed to the fullest extent of law. Open door let you out. This is no kidding matter."

Definitely sketchworthy.

We have the bus practically to ourselves, so Gramp pulls a Cheez-It—sprawls out on two seats and is snorin' like a buzz saw before we even start to move.

Purplehead conks out soon as we hit the highway, but I'm cranked to the max on Mountain Dew. While the rest of the bus is having a Z-fest and fartin' in their sleep, my mind's spinning visuals and my pencil's justa burning. They're quick and wicked rough, barely skeletons, four, five to a page, balloons, asides, notes scribbled all over the place. Derek's right— I'm a comedian with a pencil. Some are so funny I laugh while I draw. Like Leo jackknifed inside the toilet (*I was tryin' ta wipe*) and the bus buried in snow up to its windows (*Let Us Do the Driving*) and Gramp in his droopy underwear holding his pants under a men's room hand dryer (*Mug Me*). When I get home, I'll do them justice; flesh them out, add the details.

Only sketch I take my time with and that gets a whole page is Purplehead. Just thinking about our last trip to the windows makes me wanna wake her up: can already feel my heart racing. All that worrying about where I put my nose, do

I close my eyes, do I hold my breath; all that practice kissing my hand in Gramp's bathroom mirror was for nada. Felt so right making out with her, I didn't even think about it, was like my mind and screwed-up life had left the building, like nothin' else mattered more or could feel as awesome as her lips movin' against mine. Wasn't till we got interrupted by a cop checking doors and my brain started working again that I got nervous. Started wondering, *Is she liking this? Does she think I'm good? Does my breath stink?*

And it was like she read my mind 'cause a second later, she was poppin' back an orange Tic Tac and telling me, "Relax, I have my ticket. He won't bother us."

If Frankie saw Purplehead right now, he'd think I was crazy—way her head's tilted, way her mouth's open in her sleep. He'd see the purple hair and eyebrow ring and think I'd lost it, but to me, she's more than beautiful. That's why I ain't gonna tell him, even though I'd win the five bucks we got riding on who kisses a girl first, and why I covered her up with my coat so she won't be cold, and why I don't care she's droolin' on it.

CHAPTER 18

When they shake me awake, I don't know where I am. I'm so out of it, I yell, "It's vacation—I don't hafta go to school!"

Ain't till Gramp hauls me to my feet that I realize I'm on a bus and then remember why—we're going to see Derek. But my brain's so fried that's all it can register.

I'm in la-la land, tagging behind Gramp in zombie mode when that Russian voice blasts us like a freakin' foghorn: "Last warning! Take trash and all people things!"

That wakes me up, I'll tell yuh, 'cause I ain't got my *people things*! Ain't wearin' my coat, don't have my backpack! "Shit!"

I turn around—there's Purplehead, laughing at me and carrying both. "Morning," she says. "Looking for these?"

"Thanks," I tell her. "I almost forgot 'bout you, I mean them. These." I grab my stuff from her, wanting to crawl out a window. I'm right back to being a dipwad in eighth grade. *Almost forgot 'bout you*—how could I? How did I? "Sorry. Takes me a while to wake up."

"I noticed," she says. "But no worries."

Her dad's waiting right at the gate, so sayin' good-bye is so quick and confusing, it's over before I know it. Get a hug and a "see yuh," and she's gone. One second her dad's wrapping his yardstick of an arm around her shoulders; the next, he's leading her away, that purple hair vanishing in a wave of people, mostly men with briefcases all in a big hurry and too tall for me to see over.

I stand there like a gnome, legs feelin' like rubber. I wanna press rewind, wanna be back at those windows, wanna thank 'er for listening, for teaching me to kiss, for taking some of the freakin' weight off my shoulders. But I don't even know her real name.

"You okay?" Gramp asks.

"Fine," I tell him. "Good to go."

CHAPTER 19

Derek likes to say *Life sucks and then you die*, and I'm wondering about that as I stare out the window of our next bus, the new snow already turning dirty. Don't seem right to me we got to come all this way, gotta take so many buses to see someone who should be living in my own house. Our old house. The one on Douglas Street. And it don't seem right he's gotta have a state for parents when he's got his own or that a freakin' insurance company can say how much his illness is worth.

"Philadelphia," says Gramp, pointing at the sign, but not reading the rest of it: THE CITY OF BROTHERLY LOVE.

"Maybe I shoulda been born there," I tell him. "Wouldn't hafta go through five states to see mine."

Gramp slowly nods. "I know," he says, sounding sad, looking ancient, reeking of Ben-Gay. "I won't be able to make this trip too often."

"I hear yuh," I tell him, for my mouth tastes like a garbage can and my feet are so swelled up I can't tie my sneakers, but mostly 'cause I saw how hard and painful it was for him to climb up the stairs of this bus. "Too expensive."

"Got that right," he agrees, tearing into a fresh roll of Tums. "But I never had the chance to say good-bye to your brother, so I'm glad your mother asked if I'd take you."

I certainly wasn't, but as he looks at me with those blue eyes that Derek got, that I'd always wished I had, the truth is, "So am I, Gramp. Really."

Ain't till a few hours later, when we're on our last bus and seeing signs for Trenton, that I start thinking about Purple-head again. I figure by now she's already bought some clothes and a new pair of boots. The memory of that word makes me laugh, makes me pull out my sketchbook justa see her again— but she ain't there.

I stare at the empty place where the page should be, bits of paper still clinging to the spiral like evidence. I remember wishin' I had some charcoal, at least a blunt stick to blend with instead of toilet paper and my sleeve. Remember being disappointed when I finished, and wanting to rip it up. Remember noticing the windows had somehow turned from being black to being light, that she was still sound asleep, that I'd closed my eyes thinking it'd be for just a second.

I flip through the book, seeing slices of my life, seeing Derek on the stretcher, on the bathroom floor, seeing flickers of my inappropriate humor and this journey of riding the dog, but no face with awesome cheekbones or eyes that could stare right through me and understand—*That must be really hard for you.*

After four, five times of going through the pages, I finally find it next to a sketch of a bus that's so rough I took her note for one of my own.

> These are awesome! Stole mine!
> You snore worse than your grandfather!
> Check your arm, Wolverine.
>   —Marvel Girl

I pull up the sleeve of my sweatshirt, the cuffs blackened with pencil smudge, and spot the tattoo on the underside of my right forearm, a smiley face staring at me between the digits of her phone number.

I wanna tell Gramp, but he's sleeping, so I let him. But lookin' out the window at the four-lane highway that's taking me to Derek, taking me to see my brother, I'm feeling somethin' I haven't in a long, long time—happy.

Author's Note

Many years ago, after taking a Greyhound bus from Portland, Oregon, to Portland, Maine, I informed my husband that I would use that setting and experience in a book one day; Zach's journey to see his brother provided the perfect opportunity. To refresh my memory, I took several bus rides to Boston while writing this book and, like Zach, explored and spent time in South Station.

The inspiration for this novel came from reading *Castaway Children: Maine's Most Vulnerable Kids*, which appeared in the *Portland Press Herald* during the summer of 2002. In an extensive series of articles, Pulitzer Prize journalist Barbara Walsh brought to light the atrocity of our medical insurance and health-care systems for children with mental illnesses, and the hardships of those patients' families who are faced with making their children wards of the state in order to obtain treatment for them. Walsh's articles captured my heart and my anger, and prompted me to write *Riding Out the Storm*. Originally, I'd planned to write the story from Derek's point of view, but from the very first line it was Zach's voice I heard. He took right over and made the story his own.

Since writing this book, I'm proud to say Maine has passed a law to ban annual and lifetime health insurance caps. An Act to Protect Health Care Consumers from Catastrophic Debt (LD 1620, a bill put forth by Representative Seth Berry) was signed into law on April 1, 2010, by former Maine governor John Baldacci. In regard to this law, I hope the old adage "As Maine goes, so goes the nation" holds true.

I need to thank school psychologist Jayne Boulos for her valuable expertise and my daughter Jessie for her "teacher" insight. I am also extremely appreciative of those who shared their personal stories about bipolar disorder with me, for you allowed me to better understand my characters and make them real.

Thank you to writers John Cofran, Wanda Whitten, and Rachel and Emma Deans, and to editors at Holt, Noa Wheeler and Eve Adler, and copyeditor Ana Deboo. To my former editor at Holt, Reka Simonson—thank you for your friendship, your expertise, and for always being in my corner, *especially* on this book. To my agent, Sally Brady, thank you for all your help and for taking me on after dear Upton's death. To Ma, my role model, mentor, and biggest fan—"Thank you for being my mother." And last but not least, to my husband, John, who keeps me grounded and brings out the best in me—thank you for being you.